ROOFTOPS

First published by Self Propelled Artists 2021
Copyright © Michael Barry 2021

Cover design by TowerJunkieArt/MJEB
Typesetting by Camilla Cripps Editing Services
Beta reading and editing by Suzanne Karolis, Kamaia Harkness, Lucie Ataya
Editing and proofreading by Camilla Cripps Editing Services
Published by Self Propelled Artists

Disclaimer: Rooftops is a work of fiction. Names, characters, businesses, places, events and incidents are purely fictitious. Any resemblance to actual persons, living or dead, or to actual events is purely coincidental.

Typeset in Minion
Printed and bound by Ingram Spark

Rooftops 978-0-6452272-0-8 Paperback
Rooftops 978-0-6452272-1-5 Ebook

A catalogue record for this book is available from the National Library of Australia

ROOFTOPS

BY

MICHAEL J.E. BARRY

Self Propelled Artists

I acknowledge the Gadigal people of the Eora Nation as the Traditional Custodians of the Country where I write.

I recognise their continuing connection to the land and waters, and thank them for protecting this coastline and its ecosystems since time immemorial.

I pay my respects to Elders past and present, and extend that respect to all First Nations people.

I acknowledge sovereignty was never ceded.

DEDICATION

For Jean.

And for Elsa, who always wanted me to tell her a story about dragons.

THE FAERIE CLAN

The Faerie Queen – an ancient faerie
The Werewolf – Cursed mortal; grandson of Faerie Queen

THE VAMPIRE CLAN

The Dark Queen – an ancient vampire
The Young Queen – the most beautiful woman in the world; daughter of the Dark Queen
The Servant – sister to the Young Queen
The Gargoyle – a creature born of the Dark Queen

THE CHILD

Eddy – a blessed and gentle soul; child of the Werewolf and Young Queen
Jackdragon – a fearless dragon; Eddy's twin.

PROLOGUE

Eddy's Unfinished Manuscript – New York 1929

Dan walked surefooted on the scaffolding, fearless in the dimming light.

Sixty floors below, the last rays of the sun crossed the rooftops of the old row houses.

From the corner of his eye, Dan saw movement, as if a small shape had detached itself from the façade and flitted across to where the chrome-steel eagle perched at the corner of the building, glaring fiercely out over the city.

Faintly, Dan heard a child's laughter and the slap of bare feet. How the hell did a street kid get up here?

'Hey! Hey, kid!' Dan called out. 'Oh fer the love of Mike,' he complained as he made his way around the corner in pursuit.

There, sitting with legs astride the eagle, was a small child, no more than seven years old, feet dangling in the air.

'Oh, Jaysus, kid. What the heck? Come back here,' Dan said.

The kid sniffled. 'You have to come get me, mister. I'm scared.'

'It's ok, kid,' Dan said, moving slowly towards him. 'Take my hand…you're gonna be fine. Let's get you home.'

The child reached his small hand out, still too far.

Dan took another step, stretching until he was within a finger's distance. As they touched, the child's hand began to dissolve into smoke, the face grew dark, the teeth jagged. There was a loud ringing in Dan's ears.

'Come on mister! Come play with us!' the child said and pulled him forward into the thin air.

PART 1
EDDY

CHAPTER 1
JACK'S BACK

THE FIRST THING you notice about getting out is how different it feels.

I spent almost twenty-five years in and out. I did some things I am not proud of, that's the way we were raised. I didn't get there by choice.

I barely noticed the first ten years; I was too busy surviving. I am good at that. Good at surviving.

For another ten years I was an enforcer and, eventually, a torturer.

I was good at that too.

And then, one day, it just ended. That's what happens. You wake up and you're on the outside.

You know how we told you that you were to blame for so long you believed it yourself? Well, it turns out you didn't do it.

Sorry kid, that's the hand you were dealt. It's not personal.

It's very fucking personal.

***

The ballistics for certain types of weapons are harder to trace. Some of them are easier to come by. I know these things.

It wouldn't be hard. *They* wouldn't suspect a thing.

Eddy was so broken he was harmless.

I'd walk in there, say, 'Hi!'

They'd say, 'Hey Eddy,' and I would gun the first one down. Then I would reload, chase the next one into the bedroom, and take care of them.

Then I would call the police and wait.

Years before, when someone else had threatened them, I had almost killed the guy. That was my business. For later. No one ever feared Eddy though. He was too gentle.

I didn't mention we look almost identical. Almost. In an easier life, you couldn't tell us apart. In the real world we are quite different.

Eddy had compassion.

I didn't give a shit.

Eddy was scared.

I liked it when other people feared me.

Eddy didn't want to hurt anyone.

I believe sometimes you have to kill people.

Eddy believed in people.

I don't believe everyone you meet *is* a person. They might look it, but they're not. Maybe something born of human, or something akin to it, but not *human*. And I ought to know, I am one of them.

They only understand fire. When I was with them, I was fire too. I was *what-waits-outside.*

In that world there is no grey. Only red.

Make them understand what you are, what they have made you.

And that's why they put me away.

CHAPTER 2
EDDY'S APARTMENT

WHEN I GOT to Eddy's place, he was asleep and the phone on his desk was ringing.

I picked it up before it woke Eddy. Then again, I am not sure anything could have woken him at that point.

'Y'ello,' I answered.

'I just want to know if you are coming, or not?' came a woman's unhappy voice.

Ah. Knew who this was, so I said, 'Hey, Rita?'

'Yes?' she said tentatively.

I hung up the phone. I had things to do and people to see.

To say I was delighted to be out was an understatement. I fairly vibrated with the energy of freedom. My horizons had been bounded by four walls for a long time. Bars on the windows. Locks on the doors. All the comforts of my cages.

There was a stack of pages on Eddy's desk – some book he has been working on for a decade – sunburned with red marks and black patches where words have died and been buried underneath furious overwriting. I felt the urge to read it, but not here.

Checking that Eddy was still asleep, I dressed.

Half the clothes in his closet were almost brand new. I chose something he'd never wear. Something with the markings of a venomous creature.

***

Now, I wander the streets at 3 am looking for a place to get coffee, feeling as awake as someone who began awareness at dawn and lived an unbroken day until the end of time.

Eventually I find a place in the neighbourhood, a kebab shop with seating outside in the cold, where a few late-shift taxi drivers are gathered.

With a lungful of smoke, and a cup of coffee made sometime in the previous decade and reheated ever since, I start reading Eddy's unfinished story.

***

Eddy hadn't heard much from the family since he had reached out to tell them about Cheryl's suicide.

The family stayed away from Eddy for reasons they couldn't explain, some silent bubbling energy they couldn't put their finger on.

That was where I came in.

I would always find a way back to Eddy if he needed me. And he needed me now.

Back *Then*, he wouldn't let me hurt them. I couldn't, knowing how much it would hurt him.

It would not have bothered me to kill them all; they deserved it, for what they did to him. For what they did to me.

And here I am now, stuck in this loop. I can't do it. I don't even want to do it. I don't think I ever really did. Under the circumstances, these thoughts were reasonable answers to unreasonable questions.

Why'd you bring me back, Eddy? I could have stayed where I was.

I know why. Because I made you pay for it for so long, 'cos I blamed you for it, and you just ate it 'cos you love me. But really all along I was blaming myself and you knew that too.

I can't handle the way you feel it sometimes, Ed. I can't. It's too much. No one's *this* right. And I have seen you suffer. I have *made* you suffer. And all the while you just kept on loving me.

Ah shit, Eddy, don't you know I am unlovable?

Fuck you, Eddy. Fuck you and your better-ness. Fuck you that it obliges me to act in the knowledge of it, influenced by it, you fucking asshole.

I can't hate anymore, and I hate that I can't hate. I cannot hate you for accepting this, dealing with it.

It's not fair and I want them to pay.

So, I must wake you up, Eddy.

I must wake you up and ask you what the fuck you want from me if you don't want them all dead.

**

Eddy is still asleep when I get home.

The giant window in the living room is open, the curtains blowing, as if the apartment is about to tip upside down and spill us once more out into the darkness to fly above the rooftops.

Eddy, why did you bring me back?

Eddy, why didn't you leave me gone?

Eddy, wake the fuck up.

But Eddy won't. He sleeps on, dead to the world, a small smile on his face every time I come near him. It's like he feels my presence, a drape of wings hanging in shadow above him.

Eddy sleeps nestled in the bosom of the dragon.

He has left a trail for me though. I don't even have to ask him these questions. It's all in the spill of words on his desk.

It's tonight, isn't it? Here, *Now*.

You opened this up for me, you brought me back like I brought you back.

You saved me too, Eddy. It's in these pages.

Eddy is awake now.

'You're the only one who can go back *Then*,' he says to me.

'The fuck,' I say. 'How?'

'You never left,' he says.

I know he's lying about something, though. He's still there, too. A part of him, anyway.

So now I know what the scoop is. Why I am here.

The curtains are wide apart and I can see out across the rooftops. It is a bright moonlit night, and tides of children rise into the sky.

I step towards the window and look out across the city. Someone has dipped it in silver.

The wind catches the edges of the flimsy grey curtains and I take a last look at Eddy sleeping peacefully again. I step out of the window and walk upon the moonlight.

CHAPTER 3
THE FIRST FLIGHT

OUTSIDE THE WINDOW, silvery forms are floating upwards from the rooms where children sleep, heading for where they gather high above the city, as they do each night.

As I watch, a small spectral-child passes me – a younger Eddy – and I follow him.

Dark outlines of shadow surround the child, he struggles to climb upwards to follow the others.

Reaching to touch him I feel a shock of memory.

Instead of going further into the sky, Eddy is returning to the place he travels to each night, a world filled with werewolves, vampires and demons.

In this world, he lives a story that never changes. I know he needs my help to find a way out, to find the ending.

To do this, I must pass through the dark that surrounds Eddy, to tell him his own story. Not all of it…enough of it.

I follow him into the place where he speaks in images and dreams.

***

It is the beginning of memory, an unbroken chain Eddy shares with me.

Eddy and me were prized firstborn of the second generation – born to a family of vampire and fae and raised between two queens: one dark, one light. The Dark Queen – a proud breeder of malice – and the small, wise, and wiry Faerie Queen.

Eddy was a manifestation of an archangel. His beauty was in his love.

I was in his shadow, always in his shadow.

Our sire was the eldest grandchild of the Faerie Queen, cursed as a Werewolf and doomed to hunt eternally.

Our mare, a siren and drainer of energies, was the eldest child of the Dark Queen.

The Dark Queen had escaped the medieval servitude of the old country with her four children: the Young Queen and her sister the Servant, and two sons – a human and the Gargoyle.

The Faerie Queen had chased the wind to the ends of the earth for adventure, found her true love on a steamship voyage, and raised her children in a city whose harbour could hold a thousand ships of the line.

Here, amidst the bones of the long-quiescent Rainbow Serpent, a place far too old and knowing to lend ear to something barely raised up above the fabric of existence, they settled, in this faraway village at the ends of the earth.

The lands of the Serpent were fertile, and these two rivers of power crashed into this open space and filled it.

***

Memory started early. The blues and yellows of reflections on the wall from what would later be understood to be a television. Swaddled up on the couch with the Servant and watching the flickering window of light. This was not known through eyes; it was seen, even then, from afar, as if Eddy was watching another person coming to the consciousness of being.

See yourself in this world. The white tuxedo, a costume for a child. The long, straight brown hair, as if they had wanted a girl instead.

The Family lived in two houses: one up the hill and one down at the flat part of the bay, once marshland. Here, an encouraging playground had been built for children, a great, twisting, coloured snake, a celebration of the new modern country.

Around the reclaimed marsh were football fields, open flatness edged by the lapping waves of the bay where the harbour finished.

In the distance, the grey wickerwork of the Iron Cove Bridge.

A smell of biscuits from the factory suffused the neighbourhood. Crickets sang into the night. Air fell like a blanket around the world, and it was peaceful in the dark.

The Werewolf and the Young Queen were busy in their discovered selves, and the raising of the young was left to the old.

Memories of being shuffled incomprehensibly from arm to arm, person to person.

In a peasant woman's kitchen, Eddy was stored among her infinite brood; everything seen from below, crawling among the thick calves and black dresses of the women.

Picking through the strawberry plants, the victory garden overgrowing the suburban backyard save for a strip of concrete allowing access to the laundry. Endless tomatoes and ripe figs, netted to keep the birds out. The husband's rough-worn face and battered hat, his ineffable goodness and his secret grappa recipe that produced clear bottles of illicit booze.

Great gatherings of relatives appeared at harvest-time. The house smelled of the sweet acid of tomatoes boiled in enormous vats and bottled into jars by a production line of women, who would then depart with their clinking treasure until the next year.

Christmas in the tiny new-build house down the hill. A mouthful of glass shards when you chose to eat a shiny blue Christmas tree bauble and the thrill of concern as they gently eased the pieces out of your mouth.

Shapes resolved into faces and names. Poppa is Eddy's namesake: old and cracked. The repairs of battle have left a sag in his cheek and a white interface breaking the smiling line of his lip.

A candlelit sing-along, the strange older children lumbering to-and-fro, the vista seen from above, families gathered to sing Christmas songs.

In that cool night air, ever smelling faintly of chocolate from the factory, a *presence* walked with Eddy.

Eddy knew this presence was with him, as he was with them, without knowing how to express what it meant. Eddy was a blessed, bright object.

Time was formless and eternal. The bursting of life in the neighbourhood was as bright as pillars of light into a night sky.

Even though he did not understand the world, the world was *right*. Eddy and the other children existed in the safe bays where the Parramatta River joined the harbour.

The connection to the essence of life was a sense of being present within it; water inside the wave.

CHAPTER 4

NORTH ROCKS 1976

THE BLOCKS OF land, distributed for war housing and guaranteed by blood sacrifice, had been hewn straight from Bidjigal lands.

Boxy, angled modernism, perched like a landing craft from another world atop formic acid smelling mounds of bull ants. The bush savaged back barely a few feet from the property line, where, in years to come, it was to erupt scathingly and angrily in flames, demanding the return of its space.

In this place, so close to the bones of the Serpent sloping down the hill, was a long, large room that faced out into a darkness seeded with eyes. The Serpent's children peered into Eddy's room, inwards at this newcomer, this separated spark.

A few small steps from the bundled-stick fence that divided the backyard from the gum trees, a trail merged swiftly into the bush.

To the left and right, a line of similar houses sat in niches carved in shovel loads from the raw country by yellow mechanical beasts called bobcats. Eddy thought that these were the wild animals that prowled the night and stared at him from the darkness.

There were no sweet smells in this wound; only bitter scents of bruised eucalypts and the resolute, angry buzzing of insects whose quarters had been disturbed.

Alone in the great basement room, Eddy played among towers of building blocks. He was awake in the eternal night, switching the light on to keep the prying eyes of the Serpent's children at bay.

In this time, the Werewolf was summoned to the employ of a Duke and was seldom present, bringing back silver-wrapped trophies of stale airline peanuts, which Eddy would feed to the kookaburra who landed on the rough brown palings of the bush-facing veranda.

Eddy didn't know it, but he was graced by the Serpent, who, recognising in its soft endless dream the presence of this new life, dispatched Goo-Goor-Gara to greet him each morning – Goo-Goor-Gara, who awakens the sleepers back to this world to see the fire of a new day.

The land marked Eddy, accepting him as it did not accept the white boxes in which he was installed. When he walked the paths, he was returned, unharmed, as such children are.

When the redback spider crossed his leg, he was unbitten, despite the flurry of blows from the Werewolf's shoe at the sight of it.

Days passed in heat and the redolent green-leaf smell of the bush. Local children threw rocks at Eddy, and he was whisked away to the home of the Faeries until he was healed.

When he returned, the Werewolf and the Young Queen were in uneasy alignment. There had been an argument where Eddy had attempted to take her side, begging, 'Please, Daddy, don't go,' and clutching at the Werewolf, only to be thrown across the bedroom, landing solidly against a wall.

There were tastes of vomit and rock salt and eggs. Raspberry cordial curdling milk. The rough, impossibly steep angled grit of the driveway, clad in green garbage bags and manufactured into a waterslide with a garden hose and dish soap, the coarse gravel tearing through plastic and skin with each slide.

The perpetual Australian national salute – the clink of glasses filled with alcohol. The smell of stale beer from the squat orange bins crowded with shiny aluminium cans, and the brooding anger that began to fill the long corridors of the box.

In years to come, when I sat at the side of the Dark Queen, she said to Eddy, 'When you were young you feared the dark, so your mother would turn out the lights to make you scared.'

The poison was already beginning to work from within.

In this house, the Young Queen taught Eddy of her Little Bird, who followed him and told her of every dark act he committed, every sin. That Little Bird was always watching. Always.

One day Eddy would learn this omnipresent reporting eye was a myth.

At night, the twinkling eyes of the children of the Serpent. The creak-crack of the frogs, creak-crack, and the buzz and hum of bush life.

In this time, in the bright sky, Eddy was further from the other children, at the edge of the night, somewhere near the horizon. It seemed to take him forever to find his way back to bed, but he was guided each time by Goo-Goor-Gara.

In the space that exists between the old and the new, Eddy waited, alone, in endless empty hours, until one day the Werewolf was summoned to the court of the Duke, and Eddy was taken back to the old world.

CHAPTER 5
EDDY FLIES

THEY HURT EDDY to save him.

Vaccinations, one after another until his arm tingles into numbness. Eddy sits high on the doctor's bench. The Young Queen is with him. The doctor is professionally detached. Children scream.

Eddy is already no stranger to pain.

Eddy has taken a shit in the bathtub, relaxing his bowels, fostered by the Dark Queen. This is their private, dirty little secret, like so many more to come. He will be beaten for this. It is disgusting. *He* is disgusting. She is smiling. It will be *alright*.

The coat hangers are wire, dulled grey at the edges, and they bite. They leave white triangles with a sloped shoulder like a sagging pyramid.

I, who am a traveller in this land, can do nothing but watch.

The poison is spreading. In scotch and white wine, in constant sex, and in anger. Eddy watches from outside the room as the Werewolf and the Young Queen couple, then he turns away and goes back down the stairs to his room and to his building blocks.

The energy of events peaks and now Eddy is sitting on a bench in a doctor's office and the needles have not stopped.

***

Eddy is pushed into the seat by G-forces as the great silver bird screams into the sky.

Eddy does not like flying in this world. His ears are sensitive. He trains himself to fall asleep almost instantly and to wake when they have reached altitude.

They have given Eddy a speaking book, a primitive robot. It instils words in him.

SPELL CAT.

Eddy presses the buttons to mark C-A-T.

He chases the words down their length until he reaches the limit of his cryptography. He is learning to speak the language of the adults already.

He needs to.

CHAPTER 6
NEW YORK 1978

EDDY, THE WEREWOLF, and the Young Queen have arrived in Wonderland. They are in the City of Oz. Eddy is looking up through the rear window of a yellow taxi.

Everything is colossal and the very air shimmers with the energy of the city. The buildings are impossibly tall, draped in neon by night, sparkling in the sunlight by day

The whole world walks the streets. Everyone who exists and has ever existed is present. It smells of hotdogs. Asphalt.

The Golden Arches, so rare and prized in Australia, are abundant. One of them is across the road from their apartment building, next to a newsagency that sells comics about Luke Skywalker.

In the apartment the Duke has prepared, they have left Eddy hundreds of toys. A vast array of moving and battery-operated things beyond the imaginings of a Sydney child.

This is a new lair for the Werewolf, who has been appointed captain of the Duke's guard, a great honour.

The Young Queen has never beheld this world before. She is entranced, enthralled, overwhelmed by the energy.

And the money.

Eddy is taken to a concrete box filled with children of every colour and nationality.

They teach him *The Three Bears* in French. Eddy leaves bananas in his locker and they go soft and brown and stink. He does this again and again despite being told not to, even after he has been punished for it.

He cannot remember bringing them.

***

The poison is touching everything.

The Werewolf and the Young Queen play at court.

Eddy plays in the coats left in the blacked-out bedroom.

The adults do cocaine and listen to disco.

Eddy waits by himself until they take him home.

***

It snows. Eddy has never seen snow.

Eddy is playing in the playground. One child pushes him down. Another child helps him up.

'What happened?' asks the second child.

'I was trying to play with that kid but he pushed me over,' Eddy says.

The white kid looks at the black kid, then back at Eddy, and pushes him over as well. The white kid calls Eddy a name he does not understand.

***

Eddy sticks his tongue to the lamp pole.

Running along a snowy sidewalk, Eddy knocks down an elderly man. The Werewolf and the Young Queen intercede quickly before a lawsuit ensues.

'He's never seen snow. We're from Australia!'

'Australia?'

The Werewolf buys the man dinner.

Eddy is punished.

***

They are at a Chinese restaurant. The Werewolf has caught Eddy in a lie about having done a chore. Eddy is terrified because the Werewolf has partially transformed to let him know that blood awaits, but that it is the Werewolf's pleasure to spare Eddy, for today only, because it is Eddy's birthday.

***

'Don't call me Mum, say I am your sister,' the Young Queen tells Eddy.

***

'I protected kids on the back of the bus!' Eddy says, thrilled to have played a hero. No one is listening. He waits in the board room and drinks tonic water until it is night.

'My, you are growing so fast,' the doorman says.

Eddy tells him it's the tonic water.

***

The Werewolf and the Young Queen go to Vegas. They bring back a trove of memorabilia, including bottles stamped with pictures of chiefs in headdresses and containing hokum potions proclaiming luck, sex appeal, money, and magic.

Eddy rubs a little of each one on himself, sure it will work.

***

Eddy's best friend is Matomba. Eddy's favourite day is Hamburgers on Tuesdays.

***

Outside Eddy's window is an art deco ziggurat. They call it the Chrysler Building. In truth, it is a focus of power, in a place of power.

They are extremely high up here.

At night, the city dreams in waves, sinking into a deeper trance until all that is left are sirens and the constant hum.

The eyes of the bush no longer look in at Eddy. It is *always* light outside, yellowed, with darkness pooling at the tips of the buildings where they touch the night sky.

The ziggurat rises and changes colours. Eddy watches in amazement.

Once again Eddy feels the other children around him. He opens the window easily despite his feeble strength.

The cool night air and the sounds of the sleeping city wash in through the open window and Eddy feels the burst of energy. This is vastly different to the dreaming of the Serpent, this bright, insistent pulsing.

From the windows of all the rooms where children sleep, small sparks emerge and travel up into the sky, illuminating the clouds from within, like hidden lightning.

Above the city the clouds are parted, and everyone is there. So many, so close, and they rise together.

In the great darkness the Gentle Others murmur and coo; they are pleased to see the children, a susurration, endless in form, at once singular and many.

They call to their charges:

Ooom.

It is the sound of whales, deep and unearthly, guiding, greeting, and shepherding the children.

The children fly above the rooftops, watching the world below, hand-in-hand, swirling, laughing, and plunging, together all, above the cars and the people walking, above the fields and farms, above the seas, over castles and villages, over lakes and trains, over wide savannahs, and brushy forests.

When they find people in the night, the children might fly close to them and play tricks, but mostly they fly and fly and fly, with a freedom they do not find in the world of the day.

As the sun pushes the rolling heat of the Rush-Rush forward across the planet, the children begin to descend to their bodies. Dawn edges ever closer and the Gentle Others urge them back to their day-life.

When the dawn breaks, the last remaining children drop suddenly from the sky, to wake in their beds, yawning and stretching, remembering only dreams of flying.

Not all the children wish to go back, some would rather stay in the sky than return to what awaits them.

These children are unseen and felt only as a small bitterness in the smell of the world, a feeling that, at the edge of the sun's wave, some things have chased the darkness further on.

These lost children are the creatures I am kin to, made of. And that is what I call them: *kin*.

These *kin* travel with the darkness, around the world, over the rooftops, until the night brings them back once more.

CHAPTER 7
EGGS

WHEN I WOKE up, Eddy was waiting, watching me sleep.

'You came back!' he cheered, throwing his arms around me.

'Aww, come on Eddy,' I said as he squeezed the shit out of me. You must understand, Eddy isn't small anymore. 'Jesus, Eddy, you're crushing me mate, let me breathe,' I gasped as he released me.

He sat back, smiling at me. 'I'm going to make you breakfast!' he said and ran off to the kitchen. Of course, I say 'ran'. He was sort of skipping. 'I'm gonna make eggs,' he called.

I looked around the room. I was lying on his couch, still fully dressed. My half-pack of smokes was on the coffee table and my boots were off. I sat up, groggy. Travel will do that to you.

'You hate eggs!' I called back to Eddy.

I got up from the couch feeling sore, squinted at the light and grabbed my smokes. I was going to spark one up, but Eddy doesn't smoke, and I didn't want to stink his place out, so I put it back in the pack.

Eddie's apartment was free of photos. He couldn't stand the sight of himself; something he had been trained to hate. I went to the bathroom, grateful there was at least a mirror in this apartment. By the time I was out, the eggs were ready.

'You wanna go see the family?' he asked. No warning. Just said it like that.

'Wha…Are you out of your fucking mind?' I said as I walked towards the kitchen.

'You know they would be glad to see you,' he told me as I sat and began to eat the scrambled eggs he had made. Not bad.

I shook my head. 'Come on man, I just got back, they can wait. What would we even talk about?'

Eddy clapped his hands, feeling like I had given way slightly. Where there was the smallest crack, he would exploit it.

'You can tell them all about your adventures!' he said, thrilled at the prospect.

I had some things to take care of with the family alright. Telling them where I had been was not one of them. But I didn't have the heart to tell him. He was so happy to see me, so happy at the idea of somehow fixing things, of making things right. The poor kid.

Something bothered me as I finished breakfast, with Eddy just sitting there silently, watching me eat.

'Eddy, why do you have eggs?'

'Cos you like eggs,' he said.

Then it hit me. All these years he's been buying these fucking things, keeping them, throwing them out. Just in case I show up.

You want to know why I am back to hurt the people who hurt him? *That's* why.

People like Eddy are so helpless in their capacity to love that they get used. The family could hurt Eddy all they wanted but they couldn't stop him from loving them. And neither could I.

'I'm so glad you're back,' he said and hugged me, squeezing my ribs together.

Behind me, my wings stirred uneasily, and I hugged him in reply, my talons draped across his shoulders.

CHAPTER 8
THE SECOND FLIGHT

I LEFT EDDY cleaning up in the kitchen.

Beside his desk in the living room there was a vast pile of mail Eddy was too scared to open. He would ignore the bills and they would bank up until someone yelled at him, then he'd break down and they'd yell at him more, letters in bold caps and angry red underscores, until they cut off his phone, or his light, or his water.

Then he'd pay his late fees and they'd turn it back on. He'd sit silently in the dark for a few days first though.

'Fuck, Eddy,' I muttered. Shit hadn't changed.

I ripped the letters open with a claw.

'What are you doing?' Eddy asked me when I came in for a garbage bag.

'Taking care of your shit, as usual,' I said.

He looked brow-beaten, as if he might cry.

'Oh fuck, Eddy. I'm sorry, mate.'

'I'm trying,' he said at last.

I am constantly undone by him. He has no filters. No damn mask. I had to hug him for a while so he wouldn't see me shaking my head.

After that, I put him back down to rest for a bit and started sorting through his mail. There was a lot to put right.

One letter stood out among the pile.

The Werewolf was waiting for me.

Well, waiting for someone. Or maybe not waiting. Who fucking knows?

The Werewolf was in a jar, at a crematorium that Eddy was too frightened to visit. As if to confront the remains would be to confirm something. For yes, Eddy loved even the Werewolf.

That understanding struck me hard and I howled. The yell erupted from beneath my chest and exposed my true form to the sun. I raised my snout to allow the sound to stream forth and collide with the ceiling in a vapour of darkness.

I put that letter aside. Death could wait a little longer.

Eddy lived precariously perched on the edge of what he could manage. It wasn't exactly self-sufficiency and then again, it sort of was.

None of these elements were individually hard to deal with – a toll notice, a reminder to submit his taxes. It was that simple things like paperwork made Eddy scared, made him think of death.

Of course, I knew why. I was *there* too; we just react differently to things I suppose. Eddy knew that failing meant dying.

It took me all day to clean up his place. Sorting through his piles of clothes. Putting his laundry through. All these basic things. Any idea I had of setting things right outside the apartment could wait.

Where *was* the family? What the hell were they doing leaving Eddy alone like this?

***

There's a rhythm to cleaning. To straightening. When the box is small, the world needs to be very precise. What is wrecked goes out. What is dirty gets washed. What is clean gets put away.

It is dusk by the time I am done. Eddy is awake and the fucking window is open again.

I come into the living room with a box of papers to throw out and Eddy moves away from the phone like he has been caught doing something.

'Don't throw…'

'I won't throw out anything important. I *know*,' I snap at him. This is a distraction.

I nod to the window. 'You want me to go back.'

'I'm sorry,' he says.

I put the papers down. 'I'm not.'

I bend forward, tensing my shoulders. My wings push out and open, confined in the limits of the room.

I look at him, ashen-faced and sad upon the chair.

'You stay here, mate. I got this,' I say and plunge out into the night.

CHAPTER 9
LONDON 1978 / NEW YORK 1979

THERE WAS MORE flying in the big silver-and-white bird.

'Raised on the floor of a 747,' the Werewolf bragged.

The Faerie homeland was dismal; dingy and cold.

The Werewolf, the Young Queen and Eddy were greeted by the elder sister of the Faerie Queen, even more dour than the countryside, haughty and suspicious of these brash southerners with their tans and wide grins.

But she beheld Eddy with joy, beckoning him to come to her in a field of heather. Smiling, he ran to her and she embraced him.

'Karate KICK!' Eddy yelled and kicked her in the shins.

'Horrible, wicked child,' she cursed.

The gift of a submariner's cap. Trains and long coats, yet more snow, and a giant teddy bear. People gifted tributes to Eddy for simply existing and he showered his smiles on them.

And then they were back in New York, where Eddy sang along to Papa Smurf. He had many more words now.

Eddy watched cartoons that went on for endless Saturday mornings, observing with strange fascination the heavy bosom of Wonder Woman and finding himself compelled without understanding.

Eddy's was a snow globe world, jostled and shaken, only ever settling into temporary stability.

The last snows were falling. The year was passing, and the poison was spreading.

***

There was a garbage chute in the corridor outside the apartment. A prehistoric thing that no amount of washing could cleanse. It had eaten the sins of Manhattanites for decades.

Eddy kept his eye on it as he walked past. The garbage chute stared back at him in turn, knowingly, and he would shy away from it, gripping the Young Queen's hand more tightly.

Eddy loved the Young Queen with all his heart. The Young Queen found Eddy a nuisance.

The Young Queen had chosen the Werewolf, instinctively, for his brutality and violence. She had sent him a valentine; the first kindness he had received since his return from the jungle where he had been cursed to his animal form.

There on the beach as they courted, a couple of local lads passed comment on her dark looks and the Werewolf transformed and thrashed them.

The Young Queen was instantly smitten. The Werewolf would be her guarantee of safety from the family, and from the predations of her brother, the Gargoyle.

Eddy was the price to pay for this protection.

***

The Kingdom of the Duke held many wonders.

These trappings of wealth were alluring to the Young Queen; a stronger, tastier, more powerful energy. She knew her worth, and she could parlay it.

This made the Werewolf insane with jealousy.

***

Tonight, the poison has welled up.

Eddy is hiding in his room but there is no way to avoid the sound.

This beating is heavier than usual. The screams are louder, and there is the sound of glass shattering.

Something is worse tonight.

Outside Eddy's room, in the grey leather, amidst the bottles, the Werewolf is transforming as the Young Queen casts her spells at him, pulling the change forward, wanting it to be brutal, wanting it to hurt him.

The Werewolf howls as his flesh rips free into his monstrous form. Once she has him fully enraged, he turns on her and she delights in the blows, drinking in her own pain, and gaining more power with each strike.

The Werewolf picks up her small frame and casts her against the wall, shattering a glass-covered painting. He strikes her again and again, shrieking and howling until she is a pulp.

When the Wolf aspect subsides, the Man sits with her ruin.

Looking at what he has wrought, he begins to clean up the crime scene, sweeping the smashed glass into a bag, the remains of bottles tinkling in the high uneven tones of jagged pieces.

The Werewolf drags the evidence to the door, and then down the hall to the trash chute. The trail of blood runs from the living room.

The Werewolf feeds the remains of the Young Queen into the chute, and it slams shut with a red besmirched lip, her body falling and thumping deep into the bowels of the building.

***

Eddy flew that night. Uneasily. He wanted to stay, to hide behind the blanket until he could go in search of her, to see if she was still alive.

Sleep took him unwillingly. Eddy remained at the edge of where the children gathered, colder, going far from the watchful awareness of the Gentle Others.

That night Eddy lingered; their urgings unheeded.

The more into the night he ventured, the less of the world he saw. Not so much higher, but further, among the whispers of shadows.

Out here in the cold, the so-so-deep cold, always fleeing from the edge of the Rush-Rush, were the children who never returned.

After a time, these lost children would forget the light, and in turn, become *kin*.

These *kin* cried in permanent pain, unchanging trauma, doomed to remain within it forever. And sometimes, when a child had chosen to abdicate that sense of themselves, *something* would find its way back down in their place.

These *kin* returned to where others had left space, others who preferred to remain in the dark, rather than face what being back in their bodies would mean.

Here at the edges, we called to Eddy.

> *Stay with us*
> *Stay here with us*
> *Safely with us*
> *Safe here*
> *Stay*
> *Stay*

Eddy didn't believe the whispers; even a child knows when the monster only wishes to feed.

Eddy was still Eddy though. Even as he grasped the possibility of freedom from his world, he did something that only Eddy would think to do.

He took *my* hand and held me to him and tried to offer comfort.

Kin rushed to surround him, drawn, compelled by the vast presence of this food source and, as they began to feed, they forgot the Rush-Rush of the sun's wave.

***

Eddy burst suddenly awake to the honking of traffic and a grey skyline against a bright blue morning, the sun dazzling him through the open window.

The apartment was silent. Preparing himself for the expected blood, Eddy gingerly stepped across the toys and opened the door with a practised soundlessness.

Smashed glass lay on the floor – diamonds on the carpet, blood at each facet. Eddy followed the trail out of the front door and down the corridor to the trash chute.

The chute smiled at him greedily.

Eddy did not say anything. He turned and went back towards the apartment.

I walked over and opened the chute. The blood trail continued down the inside. The Werewolf *had* done it.

I considered how I would kill the Werewolf. There were small-handled knives in the drawer that would fit Eddy's grip. The Werewolf would drink, he would pass out, and I would slit his throat.

In the *Then*, Eddy is locked out; the door has shut. A neighbour finds him in the hall and knocks on their door.

After a moment, the Werewolf opens the door with a hungover 'What?' Spotting Eddy, he blinks and grabs at him. 'What the hell are you doing out there?'

'You killed mum and stuffed her down the disposal chute,' Eddy replies.

The Werewolf jumps. The neighbour takes an involuntary step back.

The blood on the floor shines in red.

'Ah, your mum cut herself on some glass, mate. That's all. Go on, get back to bed.' Eddy shuffles forward obediently.

Sorry, mate. Thanks for that,' the Werewolf apologises to the neighbour, who, satisfied, waves, and departs with a quick pat of Eddy's head.

Eddy passes their bedroom and sees the Young Queen lying on the bed in the sheets, vibrant and rosy-cheeked from fresh sex.

Eddy observes the contradiction without comment and goes to his room.

'Jesus, what's with all the bloody sleepwalking?' the Werewolf says and then returns to his queen, and they begin to fuck again.

CHAPTER 10
THE TWO EDDYS

IT IS NIGHT when I arrive at Eddy's window. It is already open. The city feeds blue stripes of light into the darkened room. I follow Eddy across the carpet and through the shifting colours.

In the living room, the Werewolf and the Young Queen are watching a talk show on a colour TV.

Eddy is walking to the kitchen. He steps on the lever to open the lid of the small trash can, and it pops up.

The Werewolf hears running water. He gets up from the couch and goes into the kitchen.

Eddy is fumbling with the button on his pyjamas. Eddy is pissing in the trash can.

Watching the Werewolf beat Eddy again is about as much fun as I expect it to be. It is fucking dreadful.

It is not the worst of the beatings. It is worse because of where Eddy had been at the time.

Eddy has been snatched out of the sky to arrive with a crash in the middle of a stream of piss and pain.

When the piss hits your legs, you feel it staining and you know there will come a beating for that as well. You are being beaten and your reaction to the beating will earn you another beating. You know that already.

Eddy is awake and in the middle of it again, without a clue as to how he got there.

I am not allowed to interfere with this moment, much as I would like to take the half cigarette out of the Werewolf's mouth and scatter him like ashes across the ugly faded decor of the kitchen, with its smell of plastic permanent strangeness.

I cannot kill the Werewolf *now*. I am aware of what is and what will be.

I am here as witness.

Eddy, I am sorry.

I watch Eddy scream and then I realise something. Eddy is behind me. I turn around to see him.

'Jesus Ed, what are you doing *there*?'

Eddy is holding the small blanket he calls his 'binky', his pyjamas are dirty, there is snot in the corner of his nose. He is miserable.

'Oh, Eddy, mate. What the hell?' I ignore the sound of *Eddy-who-screams* as he is dragged backwards to the bathroom, with the sound of a few solid backhands thrown in for good measure.

Eddy-who-has-returned is awake and screaming and pissing himself and he doesn't know why.

I bend over next to *Eddy-in-front-of-me* and tell him not to look.

'Hey, mate, its ok, I'm with you.'

'I'm sorry,' *Eddy-in-front-of-me* says.

Behind me I can hear *Eddy-who-wails*.

'It's ok, mate,' I say in the *Then/Now*. 'It's not your fault. I still can't work out why you are here twice though.'

'I'm sorry,' Eddy says again. 'I'm sorry.'

Eddy falls into my arms, and I stand up and I carry him.

I turn around and see the Young Queen waiting in the shadows, watching as the Werewolf acts. Typical.

The Young Queen is feeding from the energy the Werewolf throws off, and from the bright skein of connection that has come back with Eddy when he was snatched from the sky.

Of course, there's something they don't know. That Eddy didn't come back alone.

The wailing is subsiding as the Werewolf blunts his anger.

Even now, the bruising is welling up on *Eddy-in-the-bathroom. Eddy-the-piss-your-pyjamas.*

Eddy-the-swelling-of-pain.

I cannot move that Eddy. It is forbidden to me.

I can walk *Eddy-in-my-arms* out, and I do, unseen.

'I'm sorry,' I whisper to *Eddy-in-my-arms.*

Eddy-in-the-bathroom is being dragged, naked, towards his bedroom. Our bedroom.

Me and *Eddy-in-my-arms* are waiting in the hall, in the darkness, watching as the Werewolf, reeking of sweat and booze, passes through us with no sense of me, shutting the door to the bedroom and damning *Eddy-in-the-dark* to his piss-stained reminder of a bed.

Eddy-in-my-arms looks into me with old eyes and says, 'I am sorry I could not save you,' and I know in that moment it is *me* in that room. In that darkness.

In through the door, it is *me* sitting, in shock, on the floor among the scattered plastic toys, the mini McDonald's station, the sharp forms of off-brand building blocks, unaware of anything other than the taste of blood and the ringing in my ears from the blow to the side of my head.

In a few minutes, the shock will lessen, and I will drift off to sleep, to wake curled up on the floor in a blanket that was not in the room when I passed out.

Eddy hands me his binky and I drape it over me.

It is easy enough to leave through the open window again, the same way I had come in. Easy, and out into the dark.

'What about him?' Eddy says, pointing back.

I smile sadly. 'I'm sorry, he has to stay there.'

'It's not *fair*,' Eddy says. I know, Eddy. I know.

I take the one child I can save, and I leave the other to the damnation I have already endured and can endure again for the sake of another.

'I'm taking you home. Hold on tight.' Eddy clutches at me, holding me, knowing that he cannot be taken from this safety.

I open myself to the night and we fly.

CHAPTER 11
JACK LIVES THERE

EDDY DIDN'T GO back on that night we flew together.

When I alighted at the window of Eddy's apartment and walked into the *Now*, *Eddy-in-my-arms* stepped down and walked over to where *Eddy-on-the-couch* was and became him, a piece returned to its place in the puzzle.

No stranger to strangeness, that was still weird to watch.

I closed that fucking window though. My night was done, and I didn't want any visitors.

I never understood why Eddy didn't join the *kin*, become like them, until now.

It's because I brought him to the one place he could truly escape to. The future.

For me, it is a strange and harsh world, your world.

So bright and vibrant. So hard and solid. So *physical*. I came into this world the way I had left it, in confusion and pain. That was the *Before*. Before I was even me. So long ago even I cannot remember it.

Eddy had gifted me his understanding, his memory, and his body. In return, in the way of the *kin*, I freed him to flee.

And so, for my pound of flesh, I paid in the currency of flesh, the vulnerability of the living.

CHAPTER 12
NIGHTFLYING

THE WEREWOLF OPENS the door to Eddy's bedroom.

Eddy stands on the ledge outside of his window, staring into the skies above Manhattan. He is wearing Winnie-the-Pooh pyjamas, watching as the great ziggurat shifts colours.

They are on the twenty-fourth floor.

The curtains are flapping around Eddy, an uncanny wind is pushing the bedroom door shut. The Werewolf must force his way into the room.

The Werewolf feels something he cannot see. This is the same instinct that kept him alive in the jungle.

His child is outside the window.

'Eddy, come away from there mate,' he says gently.

Of course, *Eddy* is extremely far away.

The Werewolf sees the yawning space outside the window, he feels the force of the spring night.

The child is moving.

The Werewolf's long arms flash forward and grip Eddy's shoulders, pulling him back into the room and placing him on the carpet beside the bed.

The child gazes blankly.

Softly, the Werewolf asks, 'Eddy, what are you doing?'

'Nightflying,' says *Eddy-who-is-not-Eddy*.

The Werewolf feels his own heart pounding, steel in the tendons of his hands, a faint trembling at the edges. He is perfectly focused. He has almost lost his son. In shock, the Werewolf pulls Eddy close.

The boy is cold, clammy, jerking like a puppet operated by an uncertain hand. Looking at him in wonder, the Werewolf smells something strange but cannot place it.

The Werewolf tucks Eddy into his bed, the child placid and unresisting.

'G'night, son,' he says and kisses Eddy on the forehead.

***

The window is nailed shut.

***

The kind-faced janitor and the nice man from the office were deeply sorry, but they had to tell Eddy's parents. The trash can was still smouldering in the boardroom.

Eddy has been playing with the only toys in the room, the huge onyx-based cigarette lighters. They are fire-spitting dragons, and the paper burns easily.

Eddy drops the burning paper into the trash can in alarm.

The trash can is plastic and has caught alight.

Eddy is now lighting fires.

Eddy will be punished again.

Eddy no longer cares about the Golden Arches, or MAD magazines.

***

It is the pleasure of the Duke that the Werewolf establishes a new kingdom, and he is ordered home.

Obediently, the Werewolf shakes the small snow globe of Eddy's world, and they begin the long, laborious journey.

***

Eddy-who-is-not-Eddy flies one more time.

On their way back to Australia, the plane lands on a tropical island to refuel. As they are taking off, flying low over water, Eddy falls asleep.

When Eddy wakes, they are still flying low over water.

Everyone on the plane is strangely silent.

He is puzzled, sure that time has passed.

The engine has exploded, the plane hurtling towards the sea, the passengers screaming in terror.

The captain has recovered control and they have doubled back to land on the tropical island.

Eddy has slept through all of this.

PART 2
JACKDRAGON

CHAPTER 13
CAL'S STORY

WHILE EDDY WAS otherwise engaged, I continued to get organised. I had things to take care of.

When I come home carrying groceries, Eddy's neighbour is leaving the apartment next door. She has been watching Eddy since she moved in. They are equal in shyness; their greeting a dropping of the eyes as they approach one another in the corridor.

There is something about her. Something that smells familiar. She is still watching me as I put the groceries in one hand and open Eddy's multiple locks.

'What's your name? I've always meant to ask,' I say to her.

She smiles in surprise. 'Cal. I'm Cal.'

Still holding the grocery bags, I shake her hand.

'I'm Jack.'

We share a smile and then I take Eddy's stuff inside.

***

Tonight, as I leave Eddy's place for the sky, I see a form hovering outside the window of the apartment next door. A Sky Child. She sees me. She is not frightened, even though she can see my black wings.

There is a trail of starlight descending from the Sky Child. I can follow these sinews of light as they blossom around her.

Through the window I can see Cal, looking over old photos as if they are pictures of someone else.

The Sky Child watches with me; they cannot enter this room, but I can. I pull on the silver threads and Cal shudders as if someone has walked over her grave.

Cal turns around and sees me, showing no alarm. I extend my claw, her small hand barely fitting around a single talon, and we rise together out through the window.

The Sky Child is ahead of us in the night sky, drawn somewhere as if on a tide.

Tonight, I am here for this.

We fly, over the rooftops.

'Where are we going?' I ask.

'To my cousin's house,' Cal tells me. 'When we were little.'

We fly and fly.

In this world there is no distance between places or events, and we descend from the sky through the window of an old house.

A great threat hangs in the air. I breathe it in deeply. My wings uncurl and my fangs emerge unbidden from my lips.

I am here as witness only.

The hallway is lit by a single bare bulb. A shadowy figure walks towards the Sky Child.

Cal watches this. She has witnessed this scene many times before.

There is a tension of the surface of water, of time, the fabric of the Universe itself.

A Bad Thing is about to happen. Again.

'No!' Cal says.

The shadowy figure moves along the hall. The Sky Child cannot move.

'NO!' Cal yells, and she steps through the wall and into the path of the shadowy figure. She has broken the barrier between the *Then/Now*.

Screaming, Cal summons a mighty kick into the centre of the shadow, and it bursts in a rain of black.

With a single motion, she scoops the child into her arms and crashes through a doorway. Running with the Sky Child, she finds a car. It's unlocked. Cal is in control of her escape.

The car starts, the Sky Child is safely strapped into the seat, and Cal slams into reverse down the driveway and out into the street.

The shadow in the realm of the house flutters into fragments. I step on one and pin it with my claw. It suppurates a black–purple ichor and dissolves into nothingness.

It takes me a single leap to shatter through the mists of this house and I follow the car as it travels instantly to one place and another, Cal growing sleepier, less aware of the journey.

The Sky Child is safe with her now, and as the Rush-Rush descends and the children fall back into their beds, Cal will wake from the most curious dream, feeling better than she has in many years, knowing that she is braver and more powerful than she believed.

And over the next few days she will look at Eddy and see a small boy holding the hand of a dragon.

CHAPTER 14
DREAMS / NOW

I DREAMED I was standing in the hallway of the apartment in New York, by the trash disposal chute. Blood was on my hands.

A silhouette was watching me.

'Hello,' I said.

'I see you,' they said.

I was surprised, so I bared my teeth and raised myself up to my full height.

'I am the great and powerful Jackdragon, terrible in aspect.' I shimmered and coruscated in the colours of a blazing sunset.

They laughed at me. 'Silly dragon.'

They approached me and touched my arm. 'Powerful yes. But you are not as terrible as you think.'

They leaned in and kissed me, standing on their toes. 'You think you're a monster, but you're really an angel.'

I look to my arm where they touch me. The scales fall away and there is fresh, bright skin and…

***

It is a recurring chore to close the fucking window.

I could hear music from outside and saw Eddy's neighbour on her balcony, watering her plants and singing.

My head hurt. Eddy was nowhere to be found. Feeling exhausted, I spent the day doing nothing. I fell asleep a few times and I woke when it was dusk and found the window was open again.

I guess it is fair to say I work nights these days.

With a light step onto the windowsill and out, I went in search of Eddy.

CHAPTER 15
GLADESVILLE 1980

THE HOUSE IN the bush is gone. The Werewolf, the Young Queen and Eddy now live in a memory of New York, a new tower in the suburbs, high up, beside the Gladesville Bridge, facing Sydney's inner harbour. In place of windows are large glass sliding doors.

Eddy, who remembers everything, remembers less of this time.

Each workday, Eddy is used in the car to provide the third person to allow the Werewolf to travel in the transit lane. The Young Queen drives, as the Werewolf is not permitted to drive himself; the authorities have punished him for drinking.

***

Eddy has not flown at night for some time.

***

The poison has spread, and even though Eddy is now back in the land of the Serpent, with the love of the Faeries closer, it is worse.

The Dark Queen has settled in a new lair at the edge of the corrupt heart of her city, ever connected to the energies in her web. Higher up on the crest of the hill, her first true demon, a Gargoyle, sits on a stone perch.

The Dark Queen lives above her cauldron in a square box with barred windows and multi-locked doors and a suicidal gas-pilot water heater in the tiny bathroom. The first-floor landing, that opens onto William Street, smells of piss and is darkened by the shadows of junkies taking refuge behind the fuse box to shoot up.

It is fitting that she is here among this. It is her way. We will be sealed in that chamber for hours each day.

Here, Eddy will light fires.

Here, Eddy will choke the Dark Queen's dog until its eyes bulge from its head and it learns to fear him.

This is where Eddy will learn that you can use alcohol to supress memory.

The Dark Queen's tired footfalls echo up the stairs. She opens the door in a cascade of rattling locks, enters, greets Eddy, and falls asleep.

Eddy is alone. Eddy is always alone.

The Dark Queen makes Eddy strip and counts the bruises. She takes a knife and threatens the Werewolf.

'Leave him alone!' she says in the old tongue they will not teach Eddy.

They do not leave Eddy alone.

The Dark Queen has poisoned her lineage, sacrificing her own daughters without apology.

She will survive. They will survive. There is no rule but to survive.

Later, when she is weak, and I have sustained her, she will say, 'You are not strong, not like her,' and I will say, 'There are other kinds of strength.'

The Dark Queen loves Eddy and so the Young Queen punishes him in jealous spite for the Dark Queen's willingness to make him feel special, while having sacrificed her to the Gargoyle.

The Dark Queen knows that some of the bruises are not from the Werewolf; many of them are not. There are claw marks on his arms where the nails have bitten in.

***

'Not the face,' the Servant says to the Young Queen.

***

The snow globe is gone. The toys are gone.

***

Out of ease and convenience, the Young Queen and the Werewolf enrol *Eddy-who-was* into an inner-city school for the children of the wharfies living in council houses on the foreshore of Millers Point. The Education Department lists the area and school as 'underprivileged'.

Neither the Werewolf, the Young Queen, nor *Eddy-who-sleeps* know why they have been drawn to this place. They have returned from the bright, young New World to the Dreaming of the Serpent.

Eddy has come to this place by the harbour, where man has stapled the two edges of the foreshore together in the stone and iron echo of the great Port Jackson figs. In this ancient rats-nest of laneways and alleys, ghosts of the past scatter footsteps in all directions along the cobbled streets.

Much of the old, and even older, remains here, imprinted in the air. The Serpent has a place for young things to grow beyond a youthful measure of good and evil.

Eddy is walking up the long length of Observatory Hill to the highest commanding point of the ancient lands and early penal settlement.

He no longer hears Goo-Goor-Gara and the older name of this place. Instead, he feels the presence of those who remain. This lightning rod, which draws thunder from the humid air, retains the taste of *kin*.

In the old terraces. In the sandstone blocks of the walls of Argyle Street and the Cut.

Eddy, and *Eddy-who-is-not-Eddy*, are home.

CHAPTER 16
OBSERVATORY HILL 1980

EDDY'S PARENTS DROPPED him off on Kent Street, at the back of Observatory Hill, where they could do a quick U-turn and skip across the harbour bridge to their office in North Sydney.

Fifty cents in his pocket for lunch. Shorts and a blue button-up shirt. A bag with no books. Uncomfortable prescription shoes, and in front of him, a staircase roughhewn from the hill by convicts, forking into two paths. Years of exposure have left the stone coated in the slime and overgrowth of seasons past, making for a slippery ascent.

Observatory Hill is a singular protuberance over the flat part of Sydney, commanding a view across the inner and outer harbour.

This hill is the province of the Birra-Birra, the ancient Port Jackson fig, and Ngunuñ, the flying fox. At the top of the hill, the Observatory – a sandstone-walled fortress with rusted iron chains left embedded in the walls.

Beside the Observatory, a rotunda faces the back of the harbour bridge. Next to it, cannons have been left in place, the well-maintained iron hulks stamping: *this is ours*. Steel and iron. Stone and technology.

Walking the long staircase brought Eddy to the back of the hill. Turning right would lead towards the buildings maintained by the National Trust.

To his left, the Observatory and Upper Fort Street, the road leading down to the shops and The Rocks.

Eddy walked between the great fig trees with their soft fruits so delicious to the flying foxes, the gnarled, wide blades of aerial roots rising in undulating waves around the base of the tree. Eddy would learn to shelter behind these, pelting other children with figs, as children from generations past had done since the time of the Dreaming.

As he walked towards the front of the hill, the sounds of traffic became louder. Sydney wrapped itself around Observatory Hill, unable to strangle it, the harbour bridge sinking its roots into the stone beside it. The tail of the dragon.

The Cahill Expressway connects to a circular channel winding onto the bridge, carved into the sandstone of the hill, flanked by tall, dark iron railings, coated in an industrial, reflective grey paint.

The road surfs up from the city, forming a plateau in front of the hill where cars launch themselves across the harbour.

The bridge itself is a thing of power, a radiant energy gateway.

In the psyche of the locals, it is the anchor point, married to its bride, the pearl-white Opera House.

From the Hill, you can see the angled arch of the bridge, the cockatoo hair of the Opera House and, watching from the opposite shore, the laughing riot of the Luna Park clown face, the open mouth a gateway to ferris wheels and carousels.

This is the most sacred place of the European settlers.

Facing this new city and the quay, beside the park surrounding the Observatory, is Fort Street Primary, a red-brick box that houses the local children for their schooling.

Eddy is walking into the quiet, early morning playground. He sits on a long, corrugated aluminium bench seat and waits.

One-by-one, teachers arrive, shortly followed by the arrival of the first early, cheerfully giggling students, walking in easy companionship.

By eight o'clock, the playground is filled with children under the watchful eye of a teacher, who eventually notices that Eddy is oddly out of place and approaches, saying kindly, 'Hulloo there mister, and what's your name?'

'Eddy,' says Eddy.

The teacher smiles. 'You must be new to the school. Come with me, let's find your class, shall we?'

The school building has been produced by a mindset that believes functional is efficient and efficient is cheap. Rough red bricks and white internal walls.

A neat roman barrack construction with classrooms that look out over the city, flanking a long corridor, and on the other side, a small hall, and a stage. Upstairs is a second floor accessed via a wide, flat-staired staircase.

The principal's office is immediately to the left of the entrance.

Eddy is waiting, sitting on a chair, looking at the huge wooden panels with gold leaf imprints of names from years gone by: *Dux. School Champion. Those Who Have Fallen 1914 – 1918.* A run of names from a family with sporting prowess. *School Swimming Champion: Adams, C. Adams, J. Adams, M.*

In the other room, the adults are talking, a buzz of strange sounds, as they work out who this child is. Eventually, a teacher comes out to take Eddy where he is meant to be.

In this case, down the hall to 2C.

CHAPTER 17
THE MIDNIGHT BOYS

'YOU THINK YOU'RE smart 'cos you sound like a Yank,' says the fifth grader, punching Eddy in the arm.

The other kids line up and punch him in the arm, one after the other.

Eddy endures it. Eddy could endure it.

Eddy loses his American accent within days.

***

Eddy is drowning ants. He is waiting for the taxi that comes to take him to his cage.

The school is deserted, except for the last teacher waiting around until someone comes to pick up this child.

The teacher is frustrated. 'These parents…' he mutters, looking out of the window to where Eddy is sitting in a garden bed, drowning ants.

The thick, grey, lava-like bitumen of the playground is ripped open in places by the ancient Port Jackson fig trees, the Birra-Birra, which slow the heat of the summer for the creatures who eat their fruit and nest in their limbs.

Eddy has been summoned to a place of safety in this small pocket of the bush, amidst the renovating city.

Soon, the taxi arrives, and the teacher places an ever-cooperative Eddy inside it, and Eddy is taken back.

**

Eddy cannot sit down easily. The bruise is uneven in its yellow and purple, edging out from under his shorts. There are welts on his skin, small, white, rippled tears, and they press against the hard wooden school chair.

He is having trouble staying still. He will receive detention for it, but it is no matter. He will be in the school well after it closes anyway.

They hand Eddy a paper and a pencil and tell him to start writing.

> *Eddy is in the desert, dying of thirst.*
>
> *His plane came down somewhere south of Beersheba and he is mangled. The aircraft is mangled.*

Willie is dead; he is still in the rear cupola.

Eddy was in love with Willie, but he would never tell him that, and now Willie is dead.

Eddy crawls across the sand and his lips stick together. They tear as his mouth opens to call for help. The sun is without mercy.

Eddy is dying and he waits for it,
wishing for water.

***

Eddy is being walked up the long, wooden-floored corridor.

When the classes are in session it is almost silent in the hall, and Eddy can hear his patent school shoes click with each step. The sounds of the classrooms are muffled behind windows. The hall is high and cool.

The sixth grader who holds Eddy's hand is a figure of tremendous power and stature; he is an Adams. He is gentle with the small child as he leads Eddy to his fate. Eddy is used to this; he cooperates and awaits his punishment.

'Sir,' says Adams, knocking at the door.

'Ah, Adams. Is this him?' says the Head.

'Yes, sir.'

Adams releases Eddy's hand and pushes him forward.

'What is your name, child?' asks the Head.

'Spears, sir.'

'Ah, very good. Here.' The Head hands Eddy his story. Smudged pencil on blue-lined paper.

Eddy waits, looking down, standing in front of the class. Even though they appear in the aspect of children, he knows he stands before the power brokers of the yard, in long scowling rows.

'Well, read it!' the Head commands, and Eddy reads the few pages aloud.

As he reads, Eddy is in the desert again. He finishes, and then he is not.

'Thank you, Spears,' the Head says, turning to Adams. 'You may return him to his class.'

The Head turns to the sixth graders. 'Now, why can't you write like *that*?' he says crossly.

***

Eddy is given another series of dead arms that lunchtime and accepts his punishment silently, without fighting back.

Adams sees this.

'Fucken stop it or I'll fucken smash ya,' he says and takes Eddy away from the other children.

'You're all right, mate,' Adams says.

And so, Eddy was All Right.

***

There is a hierarchy in the secret world of children.

The school harbours the remnants of the Millers Point Mob, last of the great gangs of Sydney called *pushes*, descendants of convicts, pirates, robbers, thieves and cutthroats. And Eddy is one of them now.

> *The Millers Point Mob are we.*
> *The Millers Point Mob are we.*
> *We're always up to mischief*
> *wherever we may be, Oi!*

They sing as they rock the bus. The bus driver is terrified and pulls over.

The Millers Point Mob are scallywags, scamps, mischief-making larrikins, the terror of shopkeepers in The Rocks.

The Midnight Boys are the lowest rung of the sung-but-unspoken gang and includes the youngest Adams, Mad Mick, with his sagging patch of burned skin running from chest to chin, Davo 'Kovs' Kowalski, and now Eddy.

For the first time, Eddy is part of something.

***

The Argyle Cut is layered underneath terraces of concrete on-ramps and stairs leading to the harbour bridge

Carved from the sandstone of this place they call The Rocks, the Cut is a sonic chamber and the police horses' hooves clip and clop as they patrol.

Adams has the throwdowns: small bullseye-print, paper-wrapped fireworks that detonate on impact. The gang are waiting on the bridge that bisects the arch of the Cut.

'One, two, three!' Adams coordinates and the Midnight Boys lob their micro grenades down into the Cut to erupt in gunfire sounds around the horses' feet.

The horses are terrified. The police are infuriated. The Millers Point Mob have struck once more against their ancient foe.

> *One day I was in a courtyard,*
> *a copper said to me,*
> *if you belong to the Millers Point Mob,*
> *then come along with me.*
> *Grabbed me by the collar*
> *and tried to take me in,*
> *but I picked up me hairy fist*
> *and hit him in the chin, Oi!*
> *How many eggs for breakfast?*
> *How many eggs for tea?*
> *A loaf of bread as big as your head*
> *and a lousy cup of tea,*
> *Oi!*

Furiously, the police dismount and run up the long stairs to the overpass.

'Split!' commands Adams and the gang runs in every direction.

Eddy is running with Kovs. The laneways are narrow, perfect for artful young dodgers, but they have been unlucky. There is a patrol car in the street.

'Shit,' says Kovs. They have reached the flat and the cops are on foot behind them.

'Come here, you little bastard!' yells the constable. He has grabbed Kovs.

'Scarper!' Kovs spits as he is hauled backwards. Eddy kicks off into a blind alley, making pace on the cobbled streets of the back lanes of The Rocks.

A child's voice calls to him, 'In 'ere, quick.'

Eddy takes the small hand that comes from a doorway, and it pulls him inside, Eddy's heart pounding as the constable runs past.

The small child standing with him has a face smudged in dirt and coal dust.

'Thank you,' Eddy says to the child.

'I'm yer Charlie, mate. I couldn't let ya get nibbed.'

Eddy is shaking. He peers out from the doorway.

'The horneys are gone now chum, best you be off,' the lookout says and steps back into the shadows.

CHAPTER 18
EDDY'S DEAD

I MET EDDY'S landlady today. She called me a *dybbuk*. She has been fucking with him for some time.

'Pay the rent,' she said. 'You're late!'

I just smiled and smiled and smiled. 'Fix the air conditioner,' I said. 'Fix the *fucking* air conditioner,' she heard. She jumped back, suddenly seeing *me*.

'You! *You*!! Where is Eddy?'

I dropped my head and gave her that lopsided grin I can feel.

'Eddy's dead, love,' I said and shut the door.

***

I am searching for Eddy. He is elusive, but I know where he is.

I know who he is with.

The *kin* hide him. They'd like to keep him, even now, though that is beyond their power.

Eddy's phone has been ringing. That's ok. Everyone is used to Eddy being hard to contact.

I wait patiently for this to pass. I'll fetch him when he is done.

And so, with Eddy's world at my disposal, and all the freedom I could ask for, I sit on the floor of the living room, tossing a ball against a wall, more comfortable waiting than living.

CHAPTER 19
IN THE SKY

I AM IN the night sky.

I don't want to stay here. I want to find Eddy. And yet, here I am free, and there is no sense of time.

I feel terrific in this form, strong where the wings branch out from my shoulders. My talons gleam black-tipped at the topmasts of dark sails.

The starlight sparkles within me and I wait in the darkness, a creature of this place.

I can see the children rising above the rooftops, joyfully.

I hear the coo of the Gentle Others.

Because I am *kin,* I feel this. I hunger for it, this great burgeoning as the children pass into the next stage of awakening.

The world itself spins to greet this change.

Although I am vile, outcast, damned, I am drawn to it, as my kind are, as we all are.

I approach the Sky Children and the radiance becomes almost blinding. I feel it as warmth on my skin, a cool inky blackness where the fire burns.

Tonight I – who am rotten in essence – am permitted to climb.

The Gentle Others do not push me from the zone of their charges.

I rise through the midst of the schooling minds.

I hear the *Oooooohhhhhhhhhhhhh – Oooooooo* sounds of the Gentle Others.

I feel the brush of them on my skin too, as if something within me is *right* here, it is right to be sent here.

Terror overwhelms me and I feel as if I shall plummet; I startle at this thought and I forget how to fly.

I am falling. I, Jackdragon, the great and terrible, am falling. I am…

A gentle presence soothes me and brings me yet further upwards until I sit within the susurration, in the realm of the Gentle Others.

'*Oooooooooooooo,*' they say. '*Ooooooooooooooom.*'

And I hear, '*you are that which serves*,' and I am placed gently within them, drawing my mind around the space in which we exist and showing it to me.

Eddy is lost in a distant memory, like others who will become *kin* if they do not return.

'*OOOOOOOOOOM*,' the Gentle Others call.

I shudder and a piece of darkness falls from me. I see another patch of skin and the Rush-Rush of the sun pulls at me.

It is too late to fly back to the window, and yet I do not remain at the edge of the day, fleeing from it as the *kin* now do. Instead, I am pushed back down towards the earth, as if I am a child once more, leaving Eddy lost in memory.

CHAPTER 20
MILLERS POINT 1980

EDDY HAS A hustle.

His parents do not send him with lunch, so he gets to go to the shops at the bottom of Observatory Hill, opposite the Lord Nelson.

For twenty-five cents he can get a paper-wrapped pack of fish and chips. For ten cents he can get a potato scallop.

These are hot commodities in the playground. Eddy is the only one to have a pass to do this. He walks briskly up the hill to make sure the packet gets to the playground nice and hot.

It is grey today. It is often grey in Sydney. This is Eddy's favourite time.

On a grey day, you can see furthest across the harbour. The sun shines too brightly for his eyes.

At the top of the Hill, he forges on past the fortress of the Observatory and the kids playing in the park under the supervision of the teachers. Eddy doesn't stop to return the salvoes of ripe figs from the trees. Later, he will take shelter behind silvered rubbish bin lids, returning fire.

For now, he has a mission for the Mob, and he heads into the bitumen-covered playground.

Ripping open the newspaper, the Midnight Boys cluster around the sweet-spicy smell of salt and vinegar on the hot chips, this rare contraband.

The Midnight Boys bite at the hot scallops, in order of rank, burning and kissing their fingers at each bite. Eddy has a place in the world.

***

There is a little more freedom for Eddy now. He is allowed to make his own way back to the cage each day.

The Dark Queen has chased the Werewolf around the shop with a knife, threatening to stab him if he strikes the child again.

'Not the face.'

Eddy walks through the long connecting tunnels under the bridge, down the stairs beside the Cut where each step touches stone shaped by hand.

He passes the repainted façades and new shops at the bottom of George Street, past the Fortune of War and down to Circular Quay, where the ferries dock underneath the Cahill Expressway, a binding ribbon of steel and concrete across the throat of the city.

Eddy takes the 324 bus to Watsons Bay, but he must never get off at the stop after Nan's. That is the city's forbidden world of pleasure and pain, the beating heart of the beast.

Eddy is learning to read stories. He is reading a science fiction collection from Isaac Asimov.

> *Outside the bunker after a nuclear war, a little girl is dying from radiation. Eddy knows what it is to die. He cries for the little girl and her paper sunflower coloured in crayon, knowing she will never see a real flower, and that she is dying even now.*

Eddy knows these things.

He has missed his stop though – and now he must get out among the villains.

Eddy is at the edge of Kings Cross, where each night the whores will line up and down William Street until dawn, prostitutes of the temple of Sydney.

Eddy is crossing the road beneath the great, glowing *Coke-a-Cola* sign that sits like modern rock art over the city, here at the intersection with the street they call 'The Wall', which connects the Cross to Darlinghurst.

Kings Cross focuses the pent-up sensual energy of the city in a few blocks.

Here in the Cross everything is known, everything permitted, and, subject to the licence of the local constabulary, available.

Eddy makes his way carefully through the predatory eyes of this jungle. It is daylight though and he is safe.

He escapes unharmed from the danger zone and obediently returns to the flat above the business fronts on William Street, where the Dark Queen has come to setup shop, here in the centre of the web.

That night, he looks out through the bars on the window at the flickering signs above the ZOO Disco.

He leaves the room lights off.

Eddy falls asleep but cannot fly.

***

The Midnight Boys break into warehouses. The older ones fence the stolen items. A few parents turn a blind eye or accept 'fortuitously' found objects.

They cut strips from old tyres and they whip the pigeons with them.

Eddy is banned from the general store. He is innocent but the shopkeeper knows who he runs with. The adults act oblivious to the ways of the children – this is Sydney, and crime has been a community enterprise since its founding.

The Mob and the shopkeepers play a game common to the docks since Dickensian times. There are rules: distract, thieve, and then run. Split. Head for the laneways. Lose them there.

Shadows watch these things and approve.

***

The iron of the bridge is metallic grey and it sparkles. This industrial paint gets everywhere, on Eddy's hands, on his shorts as he grasps the railings and stares down into the cars stalled in the Cut.

Mad Mick has thrown his schoolbooks over the railing. It is hilarious.
Traffic leaving the city on a Friday afternoon is at a standstill. It is backing up the entrance to the bridge.

The Millers Point Mob still rules the city, make no mistake.

***

Across the short gap of the harbour, the grinning jaw of the Luna Park clown stares at Millers Point, crouching like a sphinx at the water beside the pylons next to the harbour bridge.

Eddy knows to respect the power of this place; it has consumed children in fire, barely a year past.

This is the territory of the ancient Milsons Point enemies, but there is a truce for summer and Eddy is forming leaner limbs, swimming in the public pool on the foreshore.

Eddy is awarded swimming proficiency certificates. Bronze 50 Metre. Silver 100 Metre. Blue paper with shiny faux-gold foil embossing.

***

It is cracker night.

The Werewolf, the Young Queen and Eddy are at the foot of the bridge, facing Milsons Point. The fireworks are loud and dangerous. It is a time before safety goggles. The children point ball shooters at one another and play *Star Wars*.

The Salvation Army are handing out fireworks from a pile in a large cardboard moving-box. The Mob have cut a hole in the back of the box and are ferreting out the fireworks, crawling underneath the van and passing them back to the others.

The children shoot the fireworks up into the underside of the bridge and catch in gleeful hands the falling, burning parachutes and the flaming plastic men that dangle from them.

The air holds the thick, acrid smell of gunpowder and the sickly-sweet burning and pooling plastic. The children spend the night firing these weapons at one another as the confused Salvos wonder how the box of firecrackers diminished so quickly.

One child loses an eyebrow.

CHAPTER 21
DARLINGHURST 1981

EDDY IS NOT always alone in the cage. Sometimes the family store his cousins with him.

Eddy's younger cousin, the Wise One, has a cyst on the side of his neck. It will remain untreated and neglected and grow to the size of a grapefruit. It will affect his speech pattern and his father, the Gargoyle, will call him 'Stupid.'

'Hey, Stupid,' the Gargoyle will say, and the Wise One will remain silent, hiding behind a mask with a cunning that he will only reveal to me in later years, when he spells out what he knows of the family business: the whole scam, every note, every act, every safe house.

The Wise One is anything but stupid. Eddy does not know this yet. Eddy is merely glad that he is not the target for a change.

**

Eddy is strangling the Dark Queen's small, black cocker spaniel. The dog's eyes are bulging out. Eddy knows when to release the animal's throat.

**

Eddy is lonely and it is late.

The bars across the windows are wrought iron. Small pot plants sit just outside the bars on the long awning of corrugated aluminium. It is grey, dirty, like bruised steel. Rain falls on it.

**

Eddy is being punished, again. He is denied access to a TV show he desperately wants to watch, so he can talk about it with all the other children in the playground tomorrow.

Eddy needs to learn. Eddy needs discipline.

**

Eddy has been taught to beg for a clean slate.

Eddy does not know what a slate is.

**

Eddy counts straps in groups of ten.

As they are administered, he dances under them, pisses himself. He cannot dance fast enough to avoid the lash. The belt.

It is not that this punishment is needed. It is that the sight of Eddy in pain is desired by those who inflict it. Eddy's terror is sought.

'You want something to cry about?' he is asked and struck again.

Eddy is a stone.

Eddy is a rock.

Eddy has crawled so far inside himself he is no longer present, as unreactive as clay, a medium for the impression of pain.

CHAPTER 22

THEN

IT IS SUNDAY, the day the Werewolf and the Young Queen like to spend lounging in bed. Eddy curries favour by bringing his parents coffee and the paper.

Eddy has stolen newspapers from the elevator. The flats that have ordered them are marked in red: 31, 23, 13.

Eddy is not allowed to cross the big swathe of Victoria Road to get to the newsagency. He must walk underneath the Gladesville Bridge, all the way around, turning a ten-minute walk into thirty. Eddy can't stand the inefficiency. He is still sent to fetch the papers, but he may not do it by the fastest means.

On this day, Eddy goes to the elevator and takes the papers out, delivering them to his parents.

When the Werewolf gets to the last page and notices the bright scarlet numerals, darkness descends.

***

It is the school holidays. Kids are playing in the street.

Eddy has gone mad. He has been staring at a wall for two weeks.

Eddy follows the shadows of people passing by. He looks at the gap in the wallpaper where it overlaps, a torn corner edge, revealing a triangular patch of the yellow paint behind it. Eddy studies the brown paisley print in minute detail. Eddy tells himself stories.

In the hallway of the Werewolf's new lair, Eddy stands *at ease* as he has been shown, his arms clasped behind him, his legs apart, face forward.

If Eddy slips, if he changes from this position, he will be suddenly, firmly, brutally corrected with a thick ear.

Staff, carrying art proofs and concept layouts back-and-forth to the Werewolf's office, walk past Eddy, uneasily skirting the small form in the hallway. Any attempt at sympathy or care for the child is shut down or warded off with a snarl from the Werewolf. Eddy is in permanent full view from where the Werewolf sits at his desk.

Eddy stares at the wall from morning until night.

When they take him home, he stands in the hallway in the darkness. Through the slats of the venetian door that seals off the living room, he sees the Werewolf and the Young Queen watching TV.

Tonight, I wait in the darkness outside the balcony, hovering beyond the blue railing, watching unseen through the great glass doors.

Tonight, Eddy has chosen death. He has come home and chosen death.

He will disobey.

Knowing this, remembering this, I howl.

When they return to the apartment, Eddy does not go to his assigned place at the wall, in the hall, in the darkness. Eddy hides underneath his bed and waits for the beating. Soon, a hand will come and reach down under the bed, dragging him out.

The wide glass sliding doors that separate the room from the balcony are heavy, but he can manage them if necessary.

Eddy has resolved his own ending. Crawling out from under the bed, he unlocks the catch on the door. He hopes his parents will give his Lego to one of the other kids.

The doors begin to slide apart, and I am horrified. This is not meant to happen.

'Jesus, Eddy. NO!'

I fly the short distance and press my claws against the handle. I am holding back a force beyond all measure. The force of history, of desire.

As I scream in fury and horror, the glass door inches open.

I bring with me what shakes the dawn, what breaks open the vault of the heavens and I hold fast. A shadow flickers inside Eddy, peering at me through the glass, and then releases.

The light in the room switches on and Eddy bolts underneath the bed.

It is the Young Queen. She is strangely kind to him; she leads him from his room to the living room.

In the living room, the TV is on, and the Werewolf berates Eddy for his behaviour. It is time to end this punishment.

Eddy stares in defiance and the Werewolf is infuriated.

'Don't eyeball fuck *me*, mate,' he snarls, demanding that Eddy stare at him face-to-face. The Werewolf transforms and bristles.

Eddy will not budge, even knowing this act of defiance will incur retribution.

Eddy chooses death and Death acknowledges his small sacrifice.

Death whispers in the ear of the Werewolf and a grudging respect illuminates the Werewolf's face.

From the balcony, I watch on, my claws itching, my fangs bared, and I snarl too.

I'll kill the Werewolf myself as soon as I get the chance, but I cannot now. I can only watch as Eddy stares Death down one more time and is blessedly merely sent to bed.

Death nods to me, looking through the windows. I wink back.

I cannot bring Eddy with me tonight. He will not open the door.

CHAPTER 23
EDDY'S UNFINISHED MANUSCRIPT - HARRY

HARRY SLEPT IN the bus shelter at the bottom of the hill on Watson Road.

No one bothered him. Well, eventually they would. But it would take a while. Then he'd wind up back at the Matthew Talbot Hostel for a few days, and later, return to his haunts around The Rocks.

Harry existed in a small, overlooked pocket of grace at the base of Fort Street, an echo of the invisibility of the coves and thieves of early Sydney.

The kids would greet him on the way up and down the hill and Harry would snore in reply, or wave. They slipped him money and stole food for him.

They applauded when he fought off another suitor for his camping spot.

Harry lived in the same spectral plane as the children, somewhere outside the regular gaze of the adult world, the working world, the suit-and-tie world.

Meanwhile, the renovation of The Rocks was overtaking them all.

The Sirius Building rose in steady, uniform concrete blocks, the temporary housing solution for displaced locals living in the townhouses that sat in long rows across Millers Point, now being converted into Japanese tourist destinations.

The Sirius itself was designed to become a hotel as soon as the last of The Rocks' residents could be pushed out or moved along.

Wharf-front warehouses, which once stored the trade of the South Seas, now housed 4-star establishments and new homes much desired by the aspirational water-view classes.

Harry knew that the children loved him.

He did not know that it was their love that turned away the inspectors at the corner, that left the park rangers mysteriously confused about which bus stop the vagrant had been reported at.

Harry was welcomed by a city that had not yet forgotten the children of its shadows. Harry didn't know it either, but he served a purpose in this world.

Harry could still get a flagon from the Fortune of War and when he drank, he could see them all: caps and waif faces. The girl in the white dress.

Harry would nod to them, and sometimes, he would fight their invisible enemies. People driving past would see an unkempt man in ragged clothes swirling and throwing punches in the air.

In this way, unknown to the worlds except the one he was in, Harry kept his vigil, and the other misfits and homeless folk of Sydney stayed away, at the bottom of The Rocks, by the Quay, and Harry kept the Hill.

As he slept, a small child kissed his forehead.

CHAPTER 24

KIN

COVENANT GARDENS IS an older block of apartments, built in the late seventies. The elevator seems small. I fill the whole space. It groans and clanks.

Today, I reach out to the White Witch, one of the few others who have escaped the hold of the Dark Queen. She fills me in on some of the current events of the family. Things are still fucked.

There is something soothing about small mundane actions. Sorting the canned beans from the corn. Stacking the shelves, seeing them set and ready.

I straighten Eddy's room, read his emails, log into his accounts, and check his perimeter. I feel myself adjusting to his world in small ways.

All the while, the stories travel up and down the aisles of my mind and I pay them no heed. I complete my tasks.

I feel my full size today. Eddy feels small by comparison, as if so much of him has been left in another room. I feel the heft of myself, the solidity in this world as well as the other. The form is enormous. I can see now why they recoil. Strange that people do not respond to Eddy the same way.

I am still cleaning up Eddy's life. Not the first time I have done this.

I have a dagger that Eddy keeps in his jar of pencils. The design goes back to ancient Egypt. I chose this one in years gone by because it was modelled on a Fairbairn-Sykes stiletto, and it will fit easily between ribs.

I cut Eddy's mail open with it.

I am almost on top of his bills, his unopened paperwork, his letters from The Government. I understand the terror with which he views all of this.

I remember the lines the Young Queen forced us to write out. The ten thousand repetitions of our sins. Up. Down. Across. *I will not (INSERT CRIME)* until our fingers cramped.

Stacked rows of lines on page after page of uselessness. Filling in the blanks in patterns. Making up games in our punishment. *I, I, I, will, will, will, not, not, not.*

And why did we obey? Why were we obedient?

It is not our punishment that is confusing, it is our cooperation with it.

**

Eddy has found a way, even in the *Now*, to where the Midnight Boys and their *kin* gather. He lives among them, seeing who they truly are, no matter who they pretend to be.

I can smell *kin* in this world too. We speak the same language of vengeance, of harm. I see their true form extending outside the shapes of those they inhabit.

Like all my kind, I am created for consequence and fashioned for destruction, yet my claws, Eddy's hands, are stayed by his love.

I gnash my fangs, cramped in this cell of flesh, waiting for the Dark Time.

Eddy-in-the-past is heading for puberty. Soon, he will not fly anymore, and I cannot regain him from the sky.

My window is closing. The horrors are too close. Eddy will spend decades with the *kin*, and I cannot free him without killing him.

Mercy is to not let him die in their embrace as they feed from him. The horror is not the end, the horror is the ongoing twilight.

Eddy needs to come home now. I *must* get him out of this. He has been there too long, and he won't come back.

To do so, he must cross the threshold, and that way lies pain.

There be dragons.

He is hiding from the fire of memory and I can't blame him.

I will buy him the time he needs though. Here, and in the *Then*.

No one else can drink from his cup. For all my might, all my power, all my fury, I may not even lift it, and I would perish to take but a sip.

I take Eddy's place in the *Here-and-Now* and I do his duties. No one need even know.

I know that the future affects the past, and I know what happens now plays some role in it. It is infuriating to wait, *I-who-am-free-of-time*.

As I think these thoughts, I realise I have been sitting in sunlight for an hour staring at my hand.

There is a prism on the window. It paints a rainbow onto the cream carpet, and I can interrupt it with my fingers. I hold it. I see a hand, not a claw.

Pieces of me are falling away.

For now, I know that Eddy is there and that I can reach him. I will fly tonight.

CHAPTER 25

DUX

EDDY IS SHUFFLED off to his cousins. They drive with 'Uncle' Billy.

'Uncle Billy, chuck a wheely,' they cry. It sounds like *willy*. Willy is slang for penis. It's hilarious.

Uncle Billy has a habit, a mullet, and faded blue tattoos that show time served.

The house has no inside bathroom.

***

Eddy is in the Gargoyle's lair. The Gargoyle has taken a bride who will in time escape him to become the White Witch.

Presently, she is in thrall to the Gargoyle, under the spell of the Dark Queen. She has borne him two children.

There is porn everywhere. Eddy does not understand these images, but they call to something burgeoning in him.

A cousin shows Eddy the panel behind the door that slants down to the side roof of the penthouse. Inside is a dark attic room. Eddy sees weapons, including a tripod with a machine gun mounted on it.

Eddy is terrified and makes the cousin shut the door. He does not want to know, and he knows that he does not want to know.

***

The Werewolf gives Eddy twenty dollars. A fortune. Eddy buys a model of a Spitfire and builds it. He takes it to the cousins in Newcastle. They put it on a stump and burn it.

***

Eddy is playing in the twilight with other children outside the Birkenhead pub. He runs across the road and he is grazed by the bumper of a taxi. The concerned cab-driver takes Eddy inside the pub to look for his parents. Eddy is terrified.

He knows he will be beaten for causing a nuisance. He is more worried about his parents finding out than he is about being hurt.

Instead, the Werewolf shows concern. The Young Queen shows concern. Eddy does not understand why.

There is no causality in this world and Eddy cannot make sense of it.

***

Each workday, the Werewolf, the Young Queen and Eddy travel across the Pyrmont Bridge. Eddy loves the quaint control house midway where the bridge parts to allow vessels through.

There is a bus shelter just before the bridge. Hippies have been in there protesting 'No Nukes' for six months. The bus stop is adorned with peace signs and pictures of flowers.

Each time he passes, Eddy smiles and waves and they wave back. He hopes they will always be there.

***

Eddy has a routine for lunch now. He eats a rissole with tomato sauce between two slices of white bread.

He is learning a comedy sketch 'Who's on first?' and it is the funniest thing he has ever heard.

He is accepted. The small world he inhabits loves him, cherishes him.

In the golden summer afternoon, he delays his return to the cage long enough to make friends. Eddy knows the lanes and alleys now in a way that will stick with him for the rest of his life. The rounded cobbles of the streets seem soft underfoot.

From now on, every time he crosses the harbour bridge it feels like walking on lightning, a feeling of warmth, a sense of knowing he is connected to this land and place.

***

The Werewolf has pleased the Duke.

The Werewolf drives a silver Volvo and plays the Moog soundtrack of *A Clockwork Orange*.

Eddy sits in a black and silver Swedish box with the uncanny speeding version of Beethoven's *9th Symphony* playing on the tape deck.

***

It is Christmas.

The Werewolf tells the Faerie Queen and Poppa, 'I can only afford to give you a card this year,' and his grandparents smile and love him anyway.

The Faerie Queen opens the envelope. It is two tickets to the Faerie homeland.

The Faerie Queen and Poppa have never flown on a plane.

The gift is priceless, unimaginable. It is the ability to travel back in time.

The Faerie Queen is in tears. Poppa is in tears.

We are all in tears.

***

It is the end of the year. Eddy is sitting in the school auditorium. The Head calls the names that are to be inscribed on the long wooden panels where the Adamses are recorded in all their glory: *Swimming Champion. Dux.*

Eddy is distracted. They call his name three times. Eddy is the *Top Student* for his year.

Bewildered, Eddy is brought up on stage and handed a brown-covered book with gilt edges containing stories of ancient heroes, smelling of the musk of fresh paper.

Eddy is returned to his seat. He has found his place, here among the Midnight Boys.

***

The Duke is well pleased. He has seen fit to reward the Werewolf, who has purchased a home in an impressive suburb.

The Young Queen has chosen to have another child.

Eddy is withdrawn from school, uprooted, given a puppy, a new sibling, and a nanny. He is snatched from everything he knew, his bonds broken.

It is here, in this bigger house with the trundle bed, that the poison will spread, and things will get worse than they have ever been.

CHAPTER 26
TRANSFORMATION

I WAS WRETCHED today. My stomach split open from the sternum to my crotch, where the scales erupted.

Behind me, my tail, locked within for so long, burst free into this realm as well.

The body was not torn, nor discarded. It was the form within this form. The inwards eye of the outwards dragon. I felt unwell. Unsteady. A steel bar across my thighs. A sickly green feeling.

With each thrash these features continued to emerge. My spine snapped and crackled. The scales shimmered green, then gold.

I hissed, I yearned for something to fight, something to eat, to destroy.

I howled, and the walls shook. All the things like me must know I hunt here.

I am horror. I am a smoking pit from which nothing emerges, hurt in a different time, beyond all form of healing. I exist to manifest this.

And now I am free.

CHAPTER 27
APARTMENT 15

EDDY'S PHONE HAS been buzzing all day. Fuck them.

What I needed to take care of, I did by email. They can wait.

I am so fully manifest tonight that the room can barely contain me. I am only waiting for the sun to go down and for the dark to deepen.

I can see the early risers. Children do not fly until they are out of their infancy. Some do. Rare ones. Eddy was one. He had to be.

I have business in this world too. It is pressing. Not so pressing as bringing Eddy home though. I know he must do this. I know only he can do this.

We who are witness are also victim.

When the time is right, I leave the confines of the apartment and it feels glorious, as it always does, to surge into the sky.

And at that moment I am aware of the man on the ledge outside Apartment 15.

The window is open, and I can see him as he sits, swallowing pills and slugging them down with vodka. He is waiting to die. He has asked for it, prayed for it, begged for it.

Death is sitting with him reluctantly, sadly, and beckons to me.

Death is solemn, and in many ways, gentle. It is Life that is ferocious.

Death, this receiver of reluctant gifts, will cede to Life what it can, for as long as it can.

Death calls to me in a thin, faint whistling. The sound is mournful, and I understand that this is a soul Death does not yet wish to receive. I sit with the man on the ledge, and he finds himself speaking without knowing why.

He converses with me easily, as I am not really there. I am a disembodied voice from the darkness, from his own mind.

He does not notice as I pluck the small pains from him with my claw.

There is a pin in his front, he takes it out to show it to me and his chest bursts open with the sadness, pushed out from within him, expelled by a stronger golden glow beneath.

I pick at the delicacies from the stream. They are tasty. He opens his mouth and a black belch glops out, running down his face until it dissolves in the rising wind.

This same wind is picking up the edges of my wings and I feel the pull of the night.

Soon it will be time for the Rush-Rush. I don't have much longer, yet I cannot leave this meal unfinished.

I desire to reach into the shining wound and wrench out what is within.

There is no need; his heart floats free from his chest and rises between us, radiant.

He stares at it, amazed, then sees me and I nod. Death gently pushes the heart back down towards the man's chest, then, taking my claw, Death burns a scarlet ribbon over the wound, flesh sizzling where the claw touches.

The man vanishes and wakes inside his room, clutching at his solar plexus, the last place the claw welds. In the morning he will find a bruise and wonder what overcame him.

Later, he will throw out the unfinished pills and fall asleep and dream of dragons.

Death pats me and goes where it is needed.

I fly up into the sky once more. The returning children signal that the Rush-Rush is coming. I have spent the night too far from the dark.

Here is where I must now go to Eddy. To find him among the *kin* at the edge where they lurk.

CHAPTER 28
THEN

EDDY IS HIDING behind his bedroom door, holding a cricket bat, praying for the courage to swing it against the Werewolf's head.

Outside in the hallway, the Young Queen screams in outrage as the Werewolf strikes her.

The Werewolf has passed into a state beyond mere transformation. He is sick. The poison is deep.

The Young Queen has control now; it is only a matter of time before the poison destroys him.

Eddy hears a hand striking flesh.

The Werewolf beats the Young Queen and, later, she will soothe her hurt using Eddy. The Young Queen will dig her nails into his flesh until Eddy screams, and the white marks fill with returning blood.

In the hallway the shouts are louder. Eddy must come to her aid, or the Young Queen will perish.

The Werewolf will kill Eddy if he emerges. Eddy grips the bat.

Eddy is a coward.

***

They are wealthy now. There is a nanny to mind the Golden Child; the child the Young Queen wanted in the way she never wanted Eddy. The Young Queen's embrace will, in time, poison the Golden Child as well.

The nanny is a country girl: broad, athletic, Australian.

The middle-class bungalow is aspirational, its location more impressive than its size.

For the Young Queen this is still not sufficient. The house is on the wrong side of the right postcode.

***

The Werewolf is at the height of his power and anything is possible. He will build a compound, raise a football team of children. He will beat his wife until the police don't come.

He will fight with the roadworks that block his easy right-hand turn from the top of Hunters Hill, taking a shovel and pick to the wet concrete, urged on by the other drunkards of the Triple H Hotel.

He will take the family, the whole family, on astonishing holidays on the harbour, renting a boat and captaining it up the coast.

He is God, Conqueror and Fiend.

***

Eddy is alone.

Eddy likes it most when it is raining.

***

Eddy sings over the Golden Child's crib at night, until the child falls asleep.

Eddy finds it easy to love, and he loves the Golden Child.

Later, Eddy will be punished when the Golden Child has done wrong. The Golden Child will be taught that it is Eddy's role to be punished.

***

Eddy has a dog. His first. Eddy roams untended. He falls from his bike, unobserved, and walks home crying.

Drunkenly, embarrassingly, the Werewolf tries to explain the birds and the bees.

***

It is Eddy's birthday.

Except for the Faerie Queen, no one has remembered. It is a rainy, quiet, grey day.

Eddy is waiting for the surprise that must surely come, some recognition.

Alone for hours, he has been reading *The Old Man and the Sea*. He is touched by the story, and he wants to say something about how it makes him feel.

The Young Queen and the Werewolf arrive home, silently, a dark brooding between them. Eddy waits for them to say something.

***

It is night. Eddy is alone again.

Eddy has achieved a sense of loneliness that few who live among others have glimpsed.

***

The nanny has gone. The anger is higher.

The Young Queen and the Werewolf are entertaining.

The neighbour has wandered in from his pool next door, half dressed, drunk. He sees them playing cards and opens his mouth unwisely.

'Hey, did ya play Acey Deucey in Nam, Patrick? Didja? Didja? Didja?'

The Werewolf has a cigarette in his mouth. He has been drinking scotch since midday.

Smoothly, without looking, he rises from the card game and throws a single punch, lifting the neighbour cleanly up into the air and backwards to land hard on the linoleum floor.

The Werewolf sits back down at the table and plays his card.

The new middle-class friends with middle-class tastes in low-quality wine cocktails, stare in shock, mouths open.

'Your card,' says the Werewolf.

***

The next day, there will be no more after school care from the neighbours.

Eddy is not allowed to play with the kids from across the road. He is not allowed to listen to Monty Python with his friend Don, or to play *He-Man and the Masters of the Universe* with Don's little brother Jimmy.

The next time Eddy sees his childhood friend will be when Don is dying of leukaemia at Royal North Shore Hospital. Eddy will remember why he liked him so much.

***

When Eddy has transgressed, he is dragged from his bed irrespective of what time of night the sin is discovered.

He is woken from sleep and pisses himself.

***

The Golden Child has not repaired the union. The memory of New York beckons.

The Young Queen is too pretty, too valuable a commodity for the Werewolf. He can never please her. He can never fill what she herself cannot fill.

The Werewolf is destroying himself in the attempt.

***

The Young Queen has taken a lover. Finally, she has chosen an equal in vampiric nature: suave, debonair, handsome.

She is confident enough to at last feed from this. She takes Eddy with her as alibi, as protection.

She makes Eddy witness the act. Eddy pretends to sleep through it.

'I can't believe I am making love to you in the front of a car,' she says to The Lover as they indulge.

This is sex in silhouette for Eddy, watching, unable to do otherwise. No amount of shutting and squeezing his eyes can stop the sound.

Eddy wants to see.

The Young Queen has made Eddy the keeper of her secret.

If he draws breath upon it, she will be killed. He will be killed. They will all die.

If this leaks out. If this emerges. If Eddy shares this. If he asks for some guidance on what this experience means.

The Young Queen hands Eddy her life, their life, and she fucks her lover in front of him, stoking further the familial attraction she has been bred to inflict, as is the nature of the vampire kind.

This is monumentally confusing for, and harmful to, Eddy, who is now made a prisoner behind his own tongue. He is coming into adulthood, a possessor of the strangest sensation in his groin.

***

In years to come, I am restrained by Eddy, as The Lover approaches me on the stairs at the New House where the Young Queen now lives with the Prince.

The Lover has never been as close to death as he is at that moment.

The Lover emerges from the back door. He is looking down, smiling. He does not notice me.

The Young Queen has summoned The Lover to her new opulent surroundings to prove to him that she, herself, has *made* it.

I see what I see. The stairs leading down to the ground floor are old, salt-sea-air worn, deep, uneven, cleft. The iron reinforcement bars are bleeding rust through the missing concrete at the edges of the steps.

I'll toss him down the stairs and listen for the snap and landing of each concussive blow. Break his skull open like an egg. He is a dead man.

I am not defending the honour of the Werewolf; he forewent that.

But Eddy? Eddy has carried this man's burden too long.

When The Lover looks up, he startles. Perhaps he sees *me* as I see him, he is nervous. 'Errr...oh, hi Eddy,' he says.

The Lover walks quickly past me before I can escape Eddy's grasp.

I will find him now that I am back. He, and others, who must pay for what they did, lest they repeat it.

***

Eddy is drinking.

Eddy is in fifth grade.

CHAPTER 29

RITA

I WAKE UP sore, as if I have exerted myself. The window is open, of course, and the pages of Eddy's story lay scattered about the room.
Everything is out of sequence.

Someone is knocking at the door. As I stand up, I feel a pull across my shoulders, a stiffness. The knocking continues.

'Yeah, yeah,' I say to no one and close the window. I pick up handfuls of pages of print and stack them haphazardly on the desk. Yawning, I scratch, ambling to the door, pulling it open before Rita can knock again.

I smile. Rita breathes in, her hand hanging in mid-air, making a small 'o' with her mouth. I nod and close the door.

'You can't ignore me forever!' I hear her yell.

I chuckle at that. 'You'd be surprised,' I say aloud, laughing. I wasn't ready for the world to intrude just yet. My plans are in disarray.

By now, I had expected to have finally settled my scores. Instead, here I am, tidying. The nagging thoughts didn't cease though.

I look up from the pile of pages, wondering how water had splashed onto them and I see Eddy, standing there, watching me.

'Fuck, Eddy, where did you come from?' I ask, startled.

Eddy looks at me with a serious expression. 'You gotta do this. Marta's dead,' he tells me.

I already know; it is a ridiculous thing to even tell me. Even so, I open the door again.

Rita is in the hall, sitting cross legged. Waiting.

'The funeral is in two days,' she says, as I lean out into the corridor.

'I don't care,' I reply, cheerfully.

Eddy is behind me and won't let me back into the apartment. I push with all the force I can, while keeping a smile on my face.

Rita gets up.

'Come if you want,' she says and walks off.

I transform instantly, and it hurts. The transformation wrenches itself out of me, my wings colliding with the ceiling, breaking the door frame.

I take a deep, sucking gasp of air and blaze to spit my fire down the tube of a hallway and obliterate her.

I feel Eddy's hand on my shoulder, like a touch of soft rain and all my fury is spent in an instant, snuffed out.

'None of this is *Now*, Eddy, this has already happened,' I scream at him.

'I know,' he says. 'This time, it's me rescuing you.'

***

I wake up with a start, the sunlight pouring in from the windows and the pages of Eddy's book flapping around the room.

I feel the soft touch of feather and hear the gentle sound of bells.

I run for the bathroom and vomit.

CHAPTER 30

NOW AND THEN AND FURTHER

I HAVE LOST all track of time. All concept of the sequence of these pages.

***

It is *Now*.

The restaurant is swanky. It is my fortieth birthday. I stand and raise a toast to the Dark Queen.

I have just pointed out that the family *business* is still running.

'You have no proof,' she hisses at me.

'To my beloved grandmother,' I say, and the family raise their glasses.

'If you ran through the front door and out the back with the cops in pursuit, she'd say she hasn't seen you in a month.'

***

Then.

The new school is comprised of local children and the children sent there by aspirational parents from Gladesville. The locals are in the moneyed classes. The rest wish to be.

When high school comes, they will be separated into those who go to private school and those who go to the local public high, where the allure of the ritzy suburb will bring the children of aspirational parents, not knowing that those who live there send their children elsewhere.

For now, Eddy is walked through the sprawling compound of the junior school and introduced to the teachers.

A rarity, the Werewolf and the Young Queen are with him. They have become responsible. Respectable. They show up to Parent and Teacher Night.

Eddy fears and loathes these meetings.

***

Eddy is brought once more to an ancient part of the land, drawn easily into it. The school building is 'Eulbertie,' huge and sandstone, made from the strongest earth of the Sydney basin, and it breathes in and out in the sweltering summer. It is degrees cooler inside the safety of Eulbertie.

Eddy is in the special class on the second floor with a view over the field and the huge wrap-around verandas where Mr Collins tells them the story of the greedy frog who drank all the water. Eddy will feel less smart because he does not understand.

Eddy does not know any of these children. So Blonde and White.

***

Further Then.

I am standing beside Eddy. Eddy is leading the Werewolf to the Young Queen.

Eddy is five. Eddy knows where she has gone and naively takes the Werewolf to her, where she is with Uncle Phil.

Uncle Phil, and his charming, wide-smiled archetype, will reoccur.

The Young Queen has many such uncles who drop in and visit, such as Ken with the purple shaggin' wagon, so far out of his depth and yet hopeful.

Eddy does not realise what these things are.

He leads the Werewolf to her, as he is bidden. The poison has started.

***

Further Then.

The Dark Queen has taken a lover. I will later learn she has a soft spot for musicians. He is Jorge, his polyester shirt is open to a forest of chest hair protected by sacred gold medallions. His voice is basso profundo.

Jorge has a routine. He stops at the local chemist and buys a toy car each time he visits the Dark Queen.

'Here, *boy*,' he says as he hands Eddy the toy car. The Dark Queen is thrilled.

Eddy plays on the stairs in front of the apartment, a single metal tube with welded corrugated steel plates and no handrails.

'Brrm,' says Eddy.

Inside the apartment there are other sounds.

Eddy will learn to drown those out.

***

Later Then.

The Young Queen has made her decision. She begins moving against the Werewolf.

It is only a matter of time now.

On the surface, this is the peak, the pinnacle.

The Werewolf summons his friends and says, 'I have nothing to offer but bread,' and then, when his work partner, the Tall Man, responds with appropriate horror at the social predicament, the Werewolf cuts the loaf open to reveal a cooked chicken within.

He is full of tricks.

***

The Werewolf is promoting 'Larry Pickering' cherry tomato kits and risqué calendars in the courtyard of the shopping centre at Birkenhead Point. During a lull in the foot traffic, he busks with his guitar.

The Werewolf sings 'Guantanamera'.

The Young Queen despairs. What will people say?

***

Eddy's school puts on a production, everyone is involved in the musical, under the supervision of the purple puff-faced Principal, who becomes beet-red with enthusiasm.

The songs are from the 1920s. Eddy knows the words.

***

Eddy is sitting in the fourth row of *Annie* in New York.

The children sing impossibly well. Eddy is amazed.

***

Eddy washes the diapers and hangs them out.

Eddy plays with his Lego and minds the Golden Child.

There is less talk in the house.

***

Eddy flies less now. I have trouble reaching him, finding him.

The worst is yet to come, and he does not want to come back.

***

The Werewolf helps Eddy to make a costume for a school project. Eddy has trouble with his homework. He freezes and cannot complete tasks.

Eddy plays at the home of the Werewolf's partner, the Tall Man.

The Tall Man has the world's largest collection of toys and won't share.

Eddy does not understand this tall child.

***

A year is passing. The house isn't right. The car isn't right. Nothing is right. Nothing works.

Eddy is reintroduced to the family. He has forgotten them.

The Faerie Queen will live another impossible thirty years from this point in time, sustained by her simplicity. Eddy will plant and tend a garden for her.

Grace, the Faerie Queen's daughter, has schizoaffective disorder. She lives partially within the other world. Now that Poppa is gone, the Faerie Queen remains behind to tend to her and to her beloved Eddy.

It is this tether, this last precious link to the world that will lead me back to him.

***

I have found Eddy. He is at the front of the waves of night, at the far end of the dawn. He is with the children as they begin their last phases.

Something is awakening within them. New feelings.

Soon, they will cease nightflying and will drop one final time to their bodies, never to return, except in strange dreams of flying over rooftops.

The Gentle Others know this and soothe the children's fear. This is the natural order of things.

Of course, the natural order of things also includes those who don't heed the gentle sounds, those who are left behind, those who remain, and those who choose to come back through the gaps.

I float, watching Eddy in the churn. I will wait with him, wait until he rises one last time and follow him home. But Eddy lingers yet again.

I feel *kin* gathering to feed on Eddy. I tip them a wink and the Gentle Others coo louder. The *kin* retreat.

I stand watch for this version of Eddy, here in the night sky, and around him I wrap my black wings and talons.

The darkness is here, and so am I.

We must return.

We must return to what comes next: us, together this time.

We always were.

CHAPTER 31

THE TEN THOUSAND THINGS

ME AND EDDY descend through the skies, ahead of the gleaming dawn.

Below me, I see a dragon entering a room through the window, holding hands with a small child. It is Eddy and me. We have done this ten thousand times before, all the lives we have lived.

I need to get back there first, and I dive. The memories stick to my wings and slide off. I get glimpses of them.

***

I am breaking into another apartment.

Later, the Servant will fence the gold jewellery I have stolen, as if this is an acceptable part of childhood.

***

I am cleaning the toilets for a new grandpa, at the insistence of the Young Queen, who has now married the Prince and seeks to curry favour with a new family.

No one else in the family will be asked to do this task, but I am lower than the lowest and nobody notices the slight.

I am invisible.

Later, I will not be allowed to call him Grandpa, despite the training they have inflicted on me.

They change their minds.

**

The Prince is rescuing me from harm he has unwittingly enabled. He and the Young Queen are returning from their honeymoon, having left Eddy and the Golden Child to the care of the Dark Queen and the Servant.

The police are outside.

The nanny has kissed me on the lips before she betrays me to them.

If not for the intervention of the Prince, I will be jailed.

The Prince will later drag me from sleep, like so many others have done, and hit me, because I have not given the dogs water. I will piss myself.

Later still, he will punch me on the jaw, egged on by the Young Queen and unsure of how to reconcile this reality with her spells of illusion.

Later still, he will send me to kill my brother.

***

I am awake. There is a man beside my bed.

It is Bill. Bill has been out of Long Bay since Tuesday. He has been shacked up with the nanny looking after these kids while their parents are on honeymoon.

Heroin needles will be left around the house.

I have broken into more places. Bill will help me fence the radio stolen from our landlord's boat.

Bill looks at me, in the darkness. He has a mullet and blue-inked tattoos.

'Can I bang my balls on your chin?' he asks.

***

Eddy is on the bus. Eddy is drunk. Eddy is twelve.

It feels warm. He feels warm. He is drinking tequila from a pink and blue plastic children's bottle. The bus is blue, the blue pleather seats are frayed.

The bus rumbles down Victoria Road.

***

My brother has picked up a knife. He has written *HA HA HA I will kill you all* in giant letters in the sand on the beach outside the Prince's house.

The Prince and the Young Queen have summoned Eddy to come and take care of this.

I find my brother on the beach, alone.

I am perfectly calm, as my kind are. Death nods to me.

I take my brother back into the house and ask him to put the knife down. He loves me, so he does.

I am very calm as I pick him up by the throat and put him bodily through the leadlight panel of the front door.

I break the door with him and prepare to end his life, a life I have suffered for, this child I have raised. A child I have taken the beatings for.

A Sorceress is with me, she begs me to let him breathe, 'Honey, you have to let him breathe, let him breathe.'

I say to him, 'I have forsworn vengeance, so you will not harm her. If you do, call the police first and make sure they get to you before I do because I will kill you, I will be the last thing you see.'

Then I leave and Eddy comes in and he breaks down in tears.

In many ways, this is his child more than the Young Queen's.

Eddy will never forgive himself, or me.

The Young Queen makes Eddy pay for the door I have broken.

***

These are *Later* days.

Worse yet awaits me, and I make it to the threshold of the window and step inside.

Eddy is asleep on the couch, and I return the child to him. Watching as they merge. He moves, restlessly in his sleep.

He is shaking. I lay my claws across his brow, and I soothe him as best I can.

There is still more of him out there. I am so very tired now.

CHAPTER 32
SCATTERED PAGES

I DREAM.

I burn within the dream.

I am pain.

***

I have lost all order of time. There is no order. There never was.

It all happens at once; it is only human perception that shapes time so.

***

Dr S. sees me bring Eddy in.

Eddy tells her, 'I am worried about my mother. My grandmother is going to die soon and it's going to affect Mum very badly.'

Dr S. sees me. I smile. Dr S. is alarmed.

It takes her some time to understand that I will do nothing, unless it is to protect Eddy, and then there is no limit to what I am capable of.

***

The Young Queen is beating me. She is raining blows on my back.

She wants me to participate in something that Eddy will not. The Werewolf is gone. The Young Queen will tell her friends, for no rational reason, that Eddy beats her too.

Eddy-who-hides-behind-the-door would not permit that. How can she ask it of him?

So, Eddy accepts her harm, her hurt. The attacks as he gets up in the morning, the attacks when he is naked, vulnerable, towel wrapped around him coming down the corridor from the shower. But today he has asked for my help.

She wants to hurt him, and Eddy does not want to be hurt anymore.

'You're a LIAR! A CHEAT! A BULLY! A THIEF!' she screams at me.

I turn and grasp her wrists underneath her clenched fists before she can hit me again.

My wings unfurl. I feel them shake free and snap open.

With my hands clamped like vices, I walk her from Eddy's room and down the hall of the New House, the long yellow hallway decorated in professional pictures of the Golden Child and the Young Queen in Hollywood poses.

There is no picture of Eddy.

I can rip her into two pieces. I tower above her, and I am strong. So extraordinarily strong. I hold her until she understands this. Then I release her arms and turn my back to her.

She throws herself at me and strikes. I don't flinch.

I do not flinch anymore.

***

The principal is caning me.

I will not react.

He lifts his cane again and again.

He searches for the fear, the terror.

All he can do is hurt me.

No one is paying attention. People may do what they like to me.

He strikes again. He will break me.

Eddy is too far away to feel this.

I can.

Eddy hides in the long grass at the bottom of Tarban Creek.

Eventually, as they all do, the principal grows weary of such sport and is too cowardly to go further.

I will not be able to use that hand for days.

No one notices.

***

Dr C. has me stare at a light.

'You are safe,' he says in his warm, high voice.

Released from the cage, I begin to scream.

I scream for ten years.

***

The Young Queen is whipping Eddy with a wire, a silver coat hanger.

Eddy is 6'4" and he lifts weights. He leg-presses 400 kilograms.

Eddy is cowering on the floor of the rented house, screaming as the Young Queen approaches, his back is to the kitchen cabinet doors.

Eddy has slid down onto the white linoleum, and he cannot stop screaming.

He raises his hands above him to ward off the blows from the past.

The Young Queen stands above him, with a smile. She cannot help herself.

I am beside Eddy, watching in horror. I look up to her, from his eyes and I speak through his mouth.

'Is this what you wanted? Is your victory complete?'

The Sorceress says, 'Get out of the house. Get out now or I will call the police.'

The Young Queen leaves.

Eddy, on the floor, is still screaming.

***

When I wake up, I am in the apartment and Eddy is sitting beside me. He looks at me with those deep puppy dog eyes and he hugs me.

'I am so sorry,' he says. 'Please forgive me. Thank you for what you did.'

I am a little confused. 'It's ok, Eddy. I love you, you know that.'

'I love you, I'm sorry,' he says again. 'Please forgive me.'

I feel something within me begging to burn.

Eddy throws his arms around me, and I cry into the shoulder of the small child, each blackened tear falling on him and sizzling into nothingness.

CHAPTER 33
MARTA'S WAKE

THE FUNERAL IS the strangest shit I have seen, and I have seen some strange shit. None of the attendees are aware of how much their souls leak. I can see the tendrils coming out of them. They are all deeply uneasy.

The funeral is held at a church that the Dark Queen did not attend, with a priest who did not know her.

All but a few pews are empty.

The Dark Queen has been a fixture of Darlinghurst for four decades.

Despite the sheer number of people and locals she has encountered over the years, the turnout is mostly the friends of the Prince and the Young Queen.

***

I am sitting beside a hospital bed at the end of the Dark Queen's reign.

It is Christmas Eve, the holier night for her culture. She could leave the ward and go to Mum's.

'But you'd rather stay here,' I say. She smiles slyly. Never too late to keep playing the game.

'You know, when you were es-small' she says, with her strange, sibilant emphasis on the s, 'you were af-fred of the dark. Your mother, she knew this, so she would put you in the room and turn out the light.'

(IN THE DARKNESS EDDY IS SCREAMING)

How cruel this is, at the end of her life, to tussle for my affections with her daughter, as if my heart could not encompass them both.

The Dark Queen now hurts me, to hurt her daughter. I am once more territory in their proxy war.

To know one more cruelty the Young Queen has inflicted, and to know that she did it to derive pleasure from the act. The only reason for the Dark Queen to tell me is for me to hate the Young Queen for it.

Eddy would be hurt.

I smile and say, 'I am not afraid of the dark anymore, Nan.'

**

Standing outside the church, I mingle with the family. My brother has flown up from Melbourne and, instead of attending, has gone off on a bender.

The service lasts less than ten minutes. Catholics take longer to bless the opening of a packet of chips. This is downright weird.

The priest says, 'I didn't really know Marta, but I know she came from The Old Country.'

He speaks a few moments more, waves incense and then the Gargoyle and his eldest son help carry the coffin out, the cheap-looking pinewood box inexplicably plastered with pictures of Eddy and the Golden Child, a 4 am caprice of the Young Queen.

None of it makes sense.

***

I am standing outside the Dark Queen's wake, at the New-New house. I am in black.

One of the Young Queen's friends sees me and surmises that this must be the place.

The friend walks hastily past, looking at me with fear bred from the Young Queen's need for fantasy and engendered by the truth of the Werewolf. At the heart of every easily told lie is a truth.

I am once again to pay someone else's tab. The sins of the father. Maybe more. Perhaps she sees me properly and knows me for what I am, in which case, *bravo*. Well-played.

With a simple choice, I can fulfil all the lies. Make what I am called real.

***

The wake has gathered the generations descending from the Dark Queen. Eddy's relatives, my *kin*.

The Gargoyle is there with the head of his new crew. He insults his son, my wisest cousin.

'Hey, aren't you gonna say something to your father?'

'My father's not here,' the Wise One responds.

I look out on the predominantly female descendants of the Dark Queen.

They will carry her line forward. Will perpetuate the vampire clan.

I realise this is the last time I will ever see them all together. It is safe for me to leave now.

The Prince says, 'You can't go!'

I look at him. If he asks me, I will stay. He has been as much a father to me as the Werewolf. I will do his bidding. And yet he does not.

'I guess I don't have the right to ask you to do anything anymore,' he says.

As I leave, I am accosted by the family celebrity, a revenant from a time I can barely name now, among the tall spires and shimmering lights.

I am called away before I can renew the acquaintance. I am glad. I say my goodbyes and depart.

This is over.

CHAPTER 34
NOW

I AM SITTING on a yoga mat, in front of the open window.

My black suit is hung up neatly.

I am waiting. I am used to waiting.

The world is still seeking to intrude on Eddy's life. The phone rings. The mail arrives. I take care of his worldly matters.

I am waiting for the portal to the sky to open.

My fight is not here, not with these people. It is out there. Up there. With the ghosts of the past.

It is night, and I must fly.

***

Among the clouds, I cannot find him. Eddy has once more proved the slip.

The Gentle Others coo to me in recognition. I seem to catch more of the light, even in darkness. I shimmer: green, gold, red.

I am at the perimeter of the Rush-Rush. There is no sign of Eddy. No trail of bleeding ichor to lead me to him. No silvered thread.

The Gentle Others feel my pain and they coo to me, *'OOOOOOm. OOOOoooooooom.'*

They draw me closer to them, seeking to help what they do not understand, but they love so much. Even those like me.

I wait in the sky for some sort of sign. Nothing comes.

Eventually, I follow the children home to the dawn and alight at the window.

My shadow is waiting, and we merge once more, nothing accomplished, nothing done.

Yet I am so very patient, and I have waited so long. I will search again.

***

My shadow talks to me as I wait.

It is hard to be in this old place in your present self.

To see all your previous selves.

***

The phone rings and this is a call I take.

It is the Werewolf's brother, Jack. Jack is drunk. Jack cannot call the Werewolf now; the Werewolf is dead.

He reaches out to me, and for the love of the Faerie Queen and respect for the human part of the Werewolf, I take the call.

Jack speaks for a time, and I listen and commiserate. His life has never been easy either. He lives in the perpetual limbo of Grace. His partner is in and out of a hospital ward. His son is in jail.

'I'm sorry I didn't do anything,' he says, and I wonder what he is talking about. 'I was there too,' he reminds me. And I remember, he was.

The violence in silence, unobserved, except for the lashing out.

Witnesses who, years later, will confess to what they saw – the simmering discontent and the bruises below the collar. This unspoken denial that allowed repeat.

Jack calls me now because his sister Cheryl is dead too.

A year ago, Cheryl hung herself on her door, making sure she would be found by her husband. Using her body as one last hurtful tool.

She had been so angry at the Werewolf, until that last time she visited him in his ruin. There in the hospital, she beheld what was left of a God and broke down.

All her hate, all her anger, all these years of wanting to hurt him and yet still craving his attention.

'You had a terrible childhood,' Cheryl says to me in our last conversation.

I keep wondering what the fuck they are talking about.

At her funeral I will see the damage she has caused to her own offspring. I will feel the tremendous guilt of her husband, so oppressive that the demons sit upon his chest, and he cannot breathe.

Another brief wake, and afterwards, I feel the need to send this energy to the Young Queen, to tell her of Cheryl's suicide.

I will text it to her, flung like a rock, knowing the Young Queen's fear of Death. She has no need of this knowledge.

I will do it because I possess her facility to harm with words.

Among all the creations of the Dark Queen, I am, but for one other, the most dangerous of them.

I have learned the cruelty and manipulation of the Young Queen. I have inherited the physicality of the Werewolf. I am as cunning as the Gargoyle and as ruthless as the Dark Queen.

I would make each one hurt, and I have the means.

'Are you going to blackmail me?' the Servant asks.

'It was only the once.'

***

Almost all whom I have chosen to serve are gone now.

The last refuse of love is duty, and my duty is fulfilled.

Eddy, where are you?

CHAPTER 35
EDDY, THEN

THE WEREWOLF HAS left the service of the Duke and struck out on his own.

Everything he touches turns to gold.

***

The Calypso is over 100 ft long, double-masted. She has made berth in Pyrmont, at a dock with a discrete entrance a few garage doors down from the fish markets.

Sailing around the harbour, she is filled with activity.

Reggae music is pumping. A sporting team – tall, beautiful men from the West Indies – are in full social engagement with the cream of Sydney glitterati.

The Vice-Captain, with his voice like honey and his roguish smile, is fetchingly handsome. The team is in good spirits, they are victorious. Every school child in Australia knows their names and batting averages.

They engage in a food fight at the airport Hilton during their press conference. They are sponsored by an electronics company selling a new Walkman competitor. Everyone on the team has one.

Muscular fieldsman, Noble, has a lady by the hand, leading her below deck, they are both wearing headphones. 'This way,' he says, and she giggles.

Opening a cabin door, Noble sees someone on the bed and quickly withdraws.

'Sorry, mon,' he says and then pauses, realising the occupant is a small child. Despite all the hubbub, this kid is sitting below, reading.

Noble closes the door.

Eddy barely notices.

A few moments later, the cabin door opens again and Noble smiles broadly, winningly, as he hands an unopened box containing a brand new music player to the child and rubs his head.

'For you,' he says and goes back out into the corridor.

Eddy looks at the music player in joy and surprise.

**

An older child strikes Eddy across the face. Eddy is small.

The music player lays broken on the ground.

'You think you're better than us 'cos you come from Sydney,' says another kid. They spit on him.

The cousin who has arranged this setup watches on, pleased.

***

The Werewolf is hunting children.

He drives slowly around Green Valley in his silver Volvo, stalking his prey.

'Is that him?' he says.

Eddy nods. Eddy is wearing band aids on his face.

The Werewolf jumps out of the car and grabs a child.

'Right. Where's the fucken kid who hit my kid?'

Within seconds, the accomplice is confessing the location of the bully.

'Come on!' the Werewolf barks, dragging the accomplice to the car.

House, after repetitive, cheaply built, dismal brown-bricked house, pass by.

The silver Volvo pulls up and the Werewolf drags the accomplice out, releasing him as soon as he betrays the bully's location.

The Werewolf takes the outside staircase to the second floor of the townhouse two at a time, and knocks. A female voice answers and then there is shouting and screaming and the sound of crashing.

The Werewolf emerges, dragging the bully by the scruff of the neck down the stairs to Eddy.

'Eddy, c'mere!' the Werewolf commands. 'Ball up your fist.'

The Werewolf looks at the bully. The bully must be fourteen, physically large by the standards of the time. He is terrified. The Werewolf shakes him, and his body jerks from side to side like a rag doll.

The bully's mum is behind them, screaming.

'Shut up!' says the Werewolf. 'Eddy, come here.'

Eddy obeys.

'Hit him.'

Eddy does not. Eddy is scared.

'*Hit* him!' commands the Werewolf.

Eddy throws a child's punch, with no more force than an angry poke. The bully doesn't feel it. Eddy is satisfied that the matter is settled.

The Werewolf hauls the bully up by the throat, transforming in front of them.

The bully's mother is frozen by the terrible sight of this, her mouth open, time suspended.

'Next time you're gonna pick on someone your own size,' the Werewolf snarls.

The bully pisses himself.

All of Eddy's victory is forgotten.

I, who stand witness, observe.

I, who hear their unspoken words, hear.

'Only *we* may harm this child.'

I have found Eddy.

He does not want to come back anymore.

CHAPTER 36
THE LAST FLIGHT

EDDY IS ALONE. It is raining.

He comes back from the sky reluctantly. More reluctantly each time.

He wants to sleep if he can. As much as he can. It is easy to find him there.

I never expected to find him among the happy memories. There are so few. He loves them all, though they are cruel to him.

Isn't that how you show love? Accepting cruelty?

Eddy *is* loved though. The Faerie Queen will remain many years yet, she will be the thread that holds him back from complete submersion in the awfulness, and in turn separate me from it too.

It is time, though. In Eddy's *Now*, I am with him, at last.

'I don't want to go there,' he says, fearing where we must travel to escape from here.

'I know little one. I'm sorry,' I tell him, knowing that there is no other way.

Now I must be the one to hurt him to save him. And I won't do that. He has been hurt enough.

I have found him here hiding in his room. Eddy is looking out of his window. Outside, there are people gathered on the lawn making bids on the house. It is up for sale.

The Werewolf does not live here anymore. Soon Eddy will begin moving from place to place again, until the Young Queen remarries.

'Where are we going?' Eddy asks me. I pick him up and leap into the night sky.

'I want to show you what they do.'

***

I am digging a hole at the root of a tree in Centennial Park. This is where we will stash the heroin. It's a small buy but pure, an ounce or so. The cut with glucose will be less than our competitors; we are consolidating the market that the family will take over.

I am the Servant's servant. I rely on them for a place to live, for work.

I keep watch.

***

I am at the New House. The phone rings.

'Rita said I should call this number.'

'I don't know what the fuck you are doing mate, don't call here again,' I say and hang up.

The Prince will not be amused that his house is now a dispensary for smack.

I have already – I reframe: *Eddy* has already – said 'no' to this and quit the *family business*.

'You'll always be looking over your shoulder,' he says to the Servant.

She cannot understand how Eddy can walk away from the money.

***

It is thirty years later.

My aunt by marriage, wife to the Gargoyle, has escaped the hold of the Dark Queen and become the White Witch. I sit with her and her son, the Wise One, at the backyard table.

The Wise One, so long silent, speaks.

'Then there was the chop house in Randwick where we bagged the stuff up,' he says, and I realise I am not alone.

Together, we begin to uncover the depth of it. The safe houses. The fronts for the laundering of the cash. How all the children were used as cover, as alibis, as mules.

The White Witch realises she has been betrayed, over and over, by the Dark Queen and the Servant. She has entrusted her children to them only to see them used in this way.

We've all been used. The truth compartmentalised.

***

The Servant has sent me to do her bidding.

I am cold, thorough, and professional, as my kind are.

I have planned an escape route. I have timed this.

I have a disguise.

I am about to take my action when a small child distracts me.

'Don't,' he says. 'Don't.'

I blink, my eyes barely visible below my pulled-down cap.

It takes me a moment to realise there is no one there and I am crucially aware I have lost precious minutes in distraction. I make my exit and I am gone.

I dispose of everything, just as I had planned, and rethink my life.

***

I am taking care of business.

I am doing what must be done.

And then one day, I am not.

***

In a garden, under a great tree, a dragon cries and a small child comforts him.

'It wasn't your fault,' Eddy says to me. 'You didn't know any better.'

'It's ok, it's not your fault,' he tells me again.

I look up at him. He is still smiling at me, even though he can see every scar, every crag, every tusk on the hideousness of my face.

'We can go home now,' he says.

I am concerned. 'Are you sure?'

He hugs me. 'Yes. Yes, I am sure. You will keep *me* safe, and I will keep *you* safe.'

I look at him. 'I'd kill for you Eddy; you know that?' I tell him, and I mean it.

'No, you wouldn't,' Eddy says, 'Because *I* wouldn't. Come on, let's go. I wanna be back before Little Nana goes.'

I stand up, towering over him, my wings striking the tree. They make a brittle cracking noise and the scales begin to fall away, leaving something that is so bright that I cannot…

Before I can look further Eddy tugs my hand.

'We gotta go, it's time,' he says, and we leap into the sky.

CHAPTER 37

THE EXIT IS THROUGH THE GIFT SHOP

THE SERVANT HAS gotten Eddy drunk.

The Young Queen has started a new job and is hosting the son of her boss, who has moved to Sydney and is settling in.

Eddy is in sixth grade now and is briefly popular for having brought a new friend to school.

Eddy is drunk on creme de menthe. It is green, sweet, sickly. Kermit the drink. The Servant is pushing a child's face between her legs. It is the child of the Young Queen's new boss.

Eddy does not remember the Servant much. He is aroused, he seeks to join in. The Servant pushes him away. 'We don't do incest in this family,' she lies.

'You think I don't remember,' Eddy will tell her later.

***

Eddy is drunk as often as he can be.

***

The Young Queen has been courting suitors.

One man, from a well-known family of merchants, has a mobile phone. It is an early piece of technology. It is impressive.

The Young Queen is still a prize.

Eddy cares for the Golden Child while she dates.

***

The old house is filled with moving boxes.

Eddy has let his guard down too far. He has said something unwise. He has mentioned that the Young Queen is dating.

The Werewolf thinks there is some path to reconciliation, yet she has already chosen.

The Werewolf chases the Young Queen around the house, beating her.

'If you touch me again, I will have both your hands broken so you can't even masturbate,' she says to the Werewolf. Later she tells other people she said this. Eddy doesn't remember.

***

In the *Then*, Eddy is with me. He grips my hand.

We fly onwards. I look to my left.

Death travels with us.

***

It is a grey Christmas Day.

Eddy has bought a cheap gold chain for the Young Queen. When he gives it to her, she takes it, checks the karat, and discards it into a drawer. It is not valuable enough.

He wanted her to love him.

The Golden Child is in diapers. Eddy is twelve. They have been entrusted to the care of the Werewolf. They are visiting with the Faerie Queen, her daughter, and the Werewolf's siblings for Christmas.

These gatherings are a pathetic half-life of the once boisterous Christmas crowds. Eventually, the Werewolf grows weary and takes Eddy and the Golden Child back to his new lair.

The Werewolf now lives in a *male-divorcee-catalogue-apartment* in North Sydney, close to Eddy's old stomping ground. It is furnished in black leather and silver chrome.

The Werewolf does not have an alarm clock, so Eddy saves his pennies and buys him one for Christmas. It is the cheapest model available, but Eddy wants him to be able to wake up.

Eddy is in the apartment now.

I watch from the balcony, rain falling on black wings.

The Werewolf is mortally wounded and ill. The sickness is with him. His world is in ruins, and the Young Queen is bleeding him in vengeance.

He is still powerful though. He has a new lover with him, a blonde with her own child, younger than Eddy. The Werewolf bullies her, and Eddy, in turn, bullies the child.

Even the Werewolf's new conquest begins to feel the transformation coming. She makes a quick exit.

The Golden Child sleeps on.

The Werewolf is drinking sambuca by the wine glass.

The day has grown dark. The Werewolf, darker.

Death alights on the balcony.

'You're a fucking cunt. A little fucking cunt. That's what you are. A fucking cunt,' the Werewolf slurs at Eddy.

Death slides the balcony doors open and steps inside.

Eddy feels the shaking of the glass panel as surely as a wind across the nape of his neck.

'You're a little fucking smart arse, you little fuck,' the Werewolf says and pours another glass.

'Your fucking mother,' the Werewolf seethes in anger.

'There were always signs,' Dr S. says to me later.

'No there fucking weren't,' I respond.

'Yes, there were,' she insists, and she was right. Eddy knew them then.

Death wraps its arms gently around Eddy as the Werewolf begins to rise, hand balling up into a fist. Eddy quickly hops up and fetches another bottle before the blow can come.

Distracted, the Werewolf grabs the poison and opens it.

'A fucking *cunt*,' the Werewolf says, filling his glass.

The Golden Child is asleep in his brown plastic carry basket. Eddy looks once at him and knows he cannot retreat. While the Werewolf is distracted, Eddy creeps to the back bedroom.

A few steps softly walked across white carpet, next to the small red LEDs of the cheap alarm clock, is the phone. Eddy lifts the receiver gently and dials the Young Queen.

'Dad's been drinking, you have to come get us, please, please,' he whispers urgently.

There is a click as the other extension lifts.

Eddy feels this sound fall like a stone down a well.

The Werewolf is on the line.

Eddy hears their voices. Eddy puts down the handset.

Soon there is shouting, and then the Werewolf's voice of command issues from the living room.

'Eddy!'

Eddy knows the price of betrayal. Eddy knows he is going to die and goes out to meet his fate.

I watch from outside the room as the Werewolf strikes Eddy and then begins to berate him, in between shots from the glass.

As it gets worse, Death opens the balcony door further.

The Werewolf has decided to punish the Young Queen by taking something she prizes.

The Werewolf takes his infant son, the Golden Child, by one leg and dangles him over the three-storey balcony. He will kill *him* to punish *her*. Then he will kill Eddy, and then kill himself in knowledge of the horror of his actions.

Eddy is prepared for Death, and he walks gently, holding Death's reluctant hand.

But Eddy is not ready to cede the child.

Eddy falls to his knees, hands wrapped around the Werewolf's legs.

Eddy is sobbing a litany, pulling on the Werewolf's arm, trying to bring the Golden Child back over the railing of the balcony.

'Please Dad, please Dad, bring him back, please, please, please, please, please, please, Dad, please, please bring him back, please Dad…'

I place my hand on Eddy's shoulder. I will be here with him, no matter what happens.

I look at Death and Death shakes its head sadly.

Eddy has got nothing left but to beg. 'Please, Dad,' he says once more.

For a moment, the Werewolf retreats and the man within surfaces.

He brings the child back over the balcony. Eddy takes the Golden Child and goes back inside, silently.

Eddy-in-my-arms watches on.

'This is not your fault,' I say to Eddy. 'Although you will blame yourself for decades, for getting caught trying to escape.'

Eddy nods. Death closes the door behind the Werewolf and pauses by Eddy, patting him gently on the shoulder.

'Can we go now?' Eddy asks me.

'There's more,' I say. 'But you don't have to.'

Eddy looks at himself in the apartment, carrying the baby bags to the front door, emotionless and reactionless, as if he is in a trance.

'What's wrong with me?' he asks.

'You're in shock mate,' I tell him. 'It's gonna be bad for a while.'

'Will I survive?' he asks me.

'Yes mate. Yes, you will,' I reply.

'Can you take me home now, please?' he asks, and I nod.

'Sorry about Christmas, mate.'

'That's ok,' he says and nestles into my arms.

I watch as Eddy in the *Then* walks down the stairs and gets into a car driven by the Servant, who proceeds to berate Eddy for the duration of the drive home.

In an hour, Eddy will crawl under the house and sit in a pile of Lego, dissociating and bawling.

The Prince will come downstairs and offer Eddy the first kindness he has experienced in some time and

Eddy, in an act of resilience known only to children, will sniff, turn off the light in his room and go upstairs to the family.

CHAPTER 38
JACK TAKES CHARGE

I HAVE TAKEN on Eddy's world. I turn up to his work. It's new work, I quit his old job; they treated him poorly. I walk a few of them through their failings. One of his colleagues worries that I am going to assault him.

If it were not for the fact that I could have broken their brittle bones instantly, I might have considered it. Eddy's record is so clean, he could wear an assault charge.

Of course, I don't need to do that. I am responding to the energy of harm that these humans carry with them, these unwanted gifts they try to pass on to others.

I have refused many of these gifts on Eddy's behalf.

For some, I have even returned the ones they bestowed. Eddy has no need of them and neither do I.

***

The waitress is flustered. All the patrons are yelling. The manager is snapping his fingers.

She hovers at my table. 'You are doing a great job,' I tell her. Her eyes widen as she looks at me, nonplussed.

'Take a moment to recover,' I say. 'As long as you are here with me, your boss cannot fault you.'

She breathes in and she shivers. Then she smiles at me.

I smile in reply.

We are in a diner somewhere in Nebraska.

The waitress is angry. And then she is not.

My new colleague, Carpenter, looks at me.

'How do you do that?' he asks me.

Puzzled, I say, 'What?' taking a bite of my eggs.

'She was really pissed and now she isn't.'

'I dunno,' I say and shrug.

***

'Some things that happen to us become part of our story,' Carpenter tells me, when I ask about an old injury. 'And you wouldn't want to lose that part of you.'

***

It is late, we are walking through the backstreets of Newtown.

Across the narrow road, in front of the townhouses that are tightly packed together, a man and a woman are fighting. He pushes her and she falls backwards. I hear the smacking sound of her head striking the concrete.

I have crossed the road before I know what I am doing, my phone's light is on, and I am checking her skull for blood.

The boyfriend is furious, screaming at me. I check the girlfriend first. I am talking, it is Eddy's voice.

'It's ok mate, it's ok. I'm checking her head because she fell. It's ok, mate. My name is Eddy, I'm Eddy, mate. What's your name?'

Eddy keeps talking. I keep checking. She may be concussed but there is no break in the skin. I check her pupils with my light.

The boyfriend is scared, angry.

'She's ok, mate,' I say and stand up.

The woman is sobbing.

'Thank God,' she says, still at my feet, holding onto my legs.

My colleagues have run to flag down the police. I am talking the boyfriend down.

'It's ok, mate, I'm only here to check her. It's ok. My name is Eddy, what's your name?'

I keep telling him my name and asking him his. He might hit a stranger, but he won't hit Eddy. Eddy means him no harm.

The police are managing the crowds on the main street at the late-night party hotspot, they will be with me in less than two minutes from now.

The blue lights are approaching, and the man is scared. He decides to hurt Eddy and he takes a step forward. Eddy is scared.

I rise within and without and I prepare to wreak havoc.

The man sees it in my eyes, and he stops like he has hit a wall. I have lifted my foot. When I place it down, I will have no need of the police.

He falls backwards. 'It's ok! It's ok, you're just a gentle giant!' he says to me urgently.

I stand at the threshold, with his girlfriend sobbing around my feet and the swirling energies within me. A moment later the police arrive, and I give my statement.

She is tended to. He is taken into custody for questioning.

It is 3 am and I am awake for eternity.

***

Eddy does not sleep. He cannot, not as an adult. Because he has found a way back *there*.

He screams during the day, randomly. When it leaks out.

His nights are the History Channel, where the war never ends.

Eddy cannot sleep. Each time he reaches the threshold, the memory awaits, fresh and undiminished. Eddy is a time traveller, and he re-enters at his own peril where my kind fears to tread.

Wherever he travels, he feels the pull of local ghosts. He wakes, running in darkness, unsure of who he is or where he is.

And so, Eddy is home wherever he goes.

CHAPTER 39
MARSFIELD 2015

EDDY IS SITTING with a family friend who is helping him find a place to store the Werewolf.

The owner of the flat wants the Werewolf out. The Werewolf will not cooperate. The effects of dementia have made the Werewolf so confused he even allows Eddy to take his car away for 'repairs'. Eddy has driven the car over to the meeting at the coffee shop around the corner from the Werewolf's flat.

The Werewolf lives in a townhouse that opens onto a natural gully between the sprawling buildings. The small backyard is enclosed by bundled-stick fencing where native birds gather to be fed, a memory of North Rocks.

Eddy will finish this meeting and then visit the Werewolf to make sure he has groceries.

On the table of the café are catalogues with pictures of smiling white-haired men and women going about their day, extolling the virtues of the local nursing homes.

Eddy looks up and sees the Werewolf approaching. This is his local shopping centre. The Werewolf is here for as much wine as he can buy until they cut him off.

The Werewolf sees Eddy and the family friend. He sees his car.

Even in this demented, damaged state, the Werewolf bristles with power. He transforms and walks towards Eddy for their final encounter.

Eddy is terrified.

Eddy is frozen.

Everything Eddy has ever feared is here, right now.
There is a stillness in the world. A slowness. Time is mutable and thought almost eternal, each one too slow to be spoken. Every thread is laid out for Eddy's awareness.

Eddy has decided he doesn't want to die, and I am here, Eddy, I am ready.

Where Eddy would cry, I will roar.

I am aware that this is the moment of reckoning and I step forward to deliver my judgement.

In a moment from now I will kill my father.

I will lay him onto the brick pavers in front of the Chinese restaurant, next to the white plastic outdoor chairs and tables and I will beat him until he is unconscious, until blood runs from his nose, until he is limp in my hands, until he is no threat to Eddy, to Mum, to me, to anyone.

For the first time the Werewolf sees *me*, not Eddy, and steps backwards.

'Whoah, Tiny,' the Werewolf says.

For the first time, the Werewolf fears *me*. Here is where the future breaks. All the rage, all my righteous vengeance is with me and only one half a footstep from being visited on this demented, worn-out old man.

Instead of my howl of fury, it is Eddy who speaks.

'I am doing the best I can to help you and if this is how you are going to treat me, you can just get fucked,' he says and walks away.

I walk with Eddy and we get into the Werewolf's car and I drive. I surround him with my wings as best I am able. Eddy crying at the wheel.

***

Here at the edge of Eddy's world, in his memory and his compassion, I walk from room to room.

I emerge in the plastic-and-carpet architecture of officialdom. Eddy is weeping, uncontrollably, quietly. He sits before a panel of three people.

Eddy is appearing before the tribunal, to beg on behalf of the Werewolf.

The Werewolf has lost his mind to the ravages of the poison that has suppressed memories of dead eyes, opened at the grave. A child's body holding an AK-47.

Eddy has come to make sure the Werewolf will be taken somewhere with dignity.

Eddy has written a letter to the tribunal the night before to say: *Tomorrow, I will be there. I will hurt, I will react, this is my condition, but I will be there.*

And he is.

***

'You are not strong, not like your mother,' the Dark Queen says to him.

'There is a different kind of strength, Nan,' Eddy says.

***

In another room of this house of memory, Eddy is standing naked, locked outside, his glasses taken away.

'You can't send him to school without his glasses,' the Prince will say.

Eddy has been sent to stand in the long thin backyard, looked on by the neighbours, facing the river where the pleasure boats cross.

He has cooperated with this shaming. This deep shaming.

Without the violence of the Werewolf to enforce it, the Young Queen and the Servant have resorted to cruelty.

'Look at your penis! You will never satisfy a woman!' the Servant yells at him, as Eddy stands vulnerable, naked in the shower. And then, 'not the face,' to her sister, the Young Queen, in the next instant.

Those who protect Eddy, harm him.

Eddy's dog is standing beside him. Eddy is trying to use the dog to shield his wounded genitals.

At night, when he is aroused, thoughts come to him of his mother having sex and Eddy wishes to destroy himself.

***

Eddy is cleaning out the Werewolf's apartment, the nicotine of chain smoking has made everything yellow and stinking. It reeks of sadness.

On the Werewolf's desk are page after page of repeated notes. The same fragment. These five long years of the Werewolf's once-great mind slipping further and further away, memories buried under hundreds of bottles of chablis.

To get to sleep, each and every night since 1968, the Werewolf has been travelling back to the fire support base under the bunker at Nui Dat.

The Werewolf visualises the rough sandbags and the cases of Armalite rounds, and yearns for a clean, swift death and release from the fear.

He drinks until he can remember no more.

***

'HOW CAN YOU HELP HIM?' the Young Queen screams.

Eddy can't explain. He has made a promise to the Faerie Queen. A pact he will not break.

'AFTER HE RAPED YOUR AUNT!' the Young Queen lies.

'You mean when I dragged her brother off her,' the Werewolf will chuckle later, in a different time, when I confront him and tell him to go to hell.

The truth of it will disarm my fury, my indignation.

Lies, transference, projection.

Vampires.

***

The aged care home is on the phone. The Werewolf assaults the other inmates.

They have placed him in a housing facility covered in pictures of the Vietnam war.

These propaganda moments do not bother the little old ladies.

The organisation advertises these pictures in the glossy magazine promoting the retirement village.

They talk of the organisation's deep connection to ANZAC history, and recognition of the sacrifice of returned veterans by placing them in a facility covered in photos of Vietnam.

In the Werewolf's mind, he is in the sick bay in Nui Dat.

The Werewolf has finally returned to hell.

CHAPTER 40
THEN, STILL

EDDY IS HATED. Despised.

'Do you know how disgusting you are?' the girl says, devastatingly.

She is pretty in an arabesque fashion. Full lips, dark-ringed hair, olive skin. She is in the 'B' crowd, and she cannot fathom this creature.

Eddy has grown morbidly obese to stop people touching him; yet…his pretty face. He could be so handsome if he just *tried*.

'How can you be like this?' she says to Eddy.

'Why can't you be like *us*?' Eddy hears.

A year later, she will approach Eddy again and he will recoil, expecting another assault.

Instead, she will shake his hand and congratulate him for topping the English exam.

Eddy will meekly say, 'Thank you.'

***

Eddy is pursued by an older man. Dark mop-top, a striped jumper and a strange expression. Eddy sits at the bus stop in front of the empty ferry wharves at Circular Quay.

The Werewolf has arranged for Eddy to get a gig as a child model, playing boardgames at a promotion at the big Hoyts Cinema on George Street.

Eddy is by himself. It is late.

Eddy has watched the man from the corner of his eye since Market Street.

They are heading for The Rocks.

Eddy knows the back streets too well to chance them and stays to the surface roads. He crosses to the other side of George Street and uses the reflections from the windows to see if he has been followed, remembering a book he was given in hospital: *How to be a Spy*.

The man follows, crossing the road. Eddy knows this is trouble. Yet the city loves this child, it surrounds him with the late-night passers-by.

It is not until they reach the bus stop that the man makes his move, sliding closer to Eddy.

'Can we go over there and we will have a little talk and I will pay you some money?' the man says, pointing to the darkened wharves.

Eddy is terrified. He has a pen knife. It is tiny. He waves it at the man.

The man looks at the pen knife and flees.

Eddy retreats closer to an old lady at the bus stop and says, 'That man tried to take me over there.' She moves backwards a little.

***

Eddy is kissed by his friend's sister. He does not know what to do. She is angry at him for not knowing what to do.

She is older. Eddy does not know these things.

She curses him out for playing hard to get.

***

Eddy is jaywalking, crossing to the other side of the road intending to bully some child.

A two-tonne box truck pulls to a sudden halt and Eddy steps behind it.

The unsecured door swings out widely and strikes him in the head. His glasses are flung from his face and blood pours everywhere.

Eddy says sorry, over and over, until an ambulance comes to get him.

He screams for his mother.

**

Eddy is in the hospital ward. He is racing in his wheelchair with another child who has been dragged by a car and is covered in scabs from face to foot.

Eddy is not punished.

The Werewolf and the Young Queen are concerned. She acts…unusually towards him. This is as close to love as she can fashion.

Eddy is given gifts, toys. The art director from the Werewolf's workplace, who had walked by him in the hall, in his punishment, draws Eddy a flip book of the accident.

Eddy's favourite gift is a book titled *How to be a Spy* and he memorises it.

**

Eddy has found his voice. He can sing like an angel.

He appears at the grand school concert. The Werewolf and the Young Queen are there; finally they will be proud.

Eddy's voice breaks during his solo. He steps off stage and a tormentor from his class points and laughs.

Eddy will not sing for some time.

**

It is Eddy's first day of high school. He is by himself. He hides with the mother of a child he knows.

**

Eddy is a bully. He is awful.

Eddy is suspended from school.

**

Eddy is sat in the centre of the room and tortured by a teacher who delights in his misery.

**

Eddy is sat outside the principal's office for three weeks writing out textbooks.

**

Eddy hides in the long grass by the park.

Eddy is absent from school for four months before anyone notices.

***

When the Young Queen marries the Prince, on the day of the wedding, the Prince's brother asks Eddy for an anecdote to tell, something funny from their past.

Eddy cannot think of one.

***

The Prince has hired three Hard Men in case the Werewolf shows up. One of them looks like a famous action-movie star.

It will be four years before Eddy sees the Werewolf again.

PART 3
ARCHANGEL

CHAPTER 41

NARRABEEN 2017

'CAN WE ADMINISTER morphine?' the doctor asks me.

We are walking more than one fine line. I don't mind the euthanasia. I mistrust the motives.

I have written to the patron of the organisation, the Governor General, to ask if the institution prioritises profit over duty. I ask him if what the Werewolf has paid in blood is enough.

In my mind, the Werewolf has already paid his due.

No one wants the Werewolf. No one wants his problems. Old soldiers never die, nor do they fade away. They terrorise the little old ladies in the nursing home and throw punches until their brain rots too much to lift an arm.

'We train them to be monsters, and then we send them home to their families,' the sad lady at the Department of Veterans Affairs tells me.

I must walk the fine line to guarantee this holding action, this rear-guard fight that will allow the Werewolf to retreat at his own pace, not at the urging of practicalities. I have been informed this room, this place in the home, is usually traded for the houses of the elderly, a princely sum.

I ask the head of their finance department: will you return with me to history? Will you stand with me in witness? If I could, I would walk with her through the jungle in the Werewolf's dreams.

CHAPTER 42
PHUOC TOY PROVINCE, VIETNAM 1968

PRIVATE SPEARS HAS his hands on his head. The RPG has exploded against a fig tree and small yellow fruits are raining down on him.

'SPEARS. GO FORWARD!' the sergeant is yelling.

'I can't, Sarge,' Spears yells back over the staccato bursts of automatic weapons.

'Why not?' the Sarge yells in reply.

'Some mad bastard's shooting at me, Sarge.'

'SPEARS!' the Sergeant yells.

Spears gives up his life, his future, his dreams of being a racing car driver, his children-yet-to-come, his mother at home going slowly mad, and steps forward from the tree he is sheltering behind.

Spears is already dead in his own mind. As dead as his best mate in the unit, Binky, who sat on a mine under a tree when they finished patrol.

With perfect focus, Spears fires rounds from the self-loading rifle, aiming for the fallen tree in front of him, knowing that the heavy 7.62mm rounds will pass easily through the foliage and on through the decaying wood.

Spears has two grenades. He lobs them over the fallen tree to where Lieutenant Truc of the NVA has been keeping Charlie Company at bay for the last fifteen minutes.

In twenty minutes, Spears will pose for a photograph in front of the headless trunk of the Lieutenant's body, bullet holes punched into it like studs in an overstuffed couch.

In six months, Private Spears will be on an aircraft carrier off the coast of Vietnam, being fed condensed milk and bread to fatten him up from his time in the jungle.

Private Spears will leave his fear there. Death will now accompany him wherever he goes.

In forty years, Private Spears (retired) will travel back to Vietnam and honour the dead, recording the day, date, and time of Lieutenant Truc's killing. The Werewolf wants the Lieutenant's family to know that he died bravely, allowing his men to escape the Australian ambush.

In fifty years, the Werewolf will awaken in an aged care facility decorated with pictures from the era of his deployment and scream for a medic.

***

Now.

I *want* the doctor to be able to administer the coup de grace, but not at *their* convenience.

The doctor is shocked that anyone would have the umbrage to refuse his decision to kill the man. The Werewolf is a vegetable. A drooling refuse of humanity, a brain cast into shadow by the excess of booze and dementia.

I do not expect the Werewolf to recover.

I want him to die when *he* chooses.

When they summon me the first time, I sing to the Werewolf. He rallies.

Cheryl, his sister, also summoned to his end, sees him. I watch her coming out of his hospital room in shock.

Twelve months earlier she sees him in the care facility; the ruin of the God.

She is horrified by her own treatment of him, the hate and anger she carried towards him for leaving her, them, the family, to deal with their mother and her madness.

She does not know the cost he has paid for cold-cocking his mother during a psychotic break.

She is angered by his incessant demands that she rejects their working-class roots. She has loved and hated him all this time. Now it is his end and all she has is regret and sadness.

In four years, she will hang herself on her door for her husband to find.

In the end, the Werewolf will pass at 2 am. I do not refuse the morphine a second time.

Of course, I am awake when the call comes in to tell me. I know what it is before the phone has rung.

***

I have organised a piper for the Faerie Queen's ninetieth birthday. He is a good piper. She cries.

I will arrange for the same piper to play her to rest in two years from now.

***

I have arranged a piper for the funeral of the Werewolf.

It is a small affair, and the celebrant won't read his eulogy, thus I do.

When it is done, I salute his coffin and leave a container of his ashes untouched at the crematorium for four years.

***

I have arranged a piper for his sister's funeral too. It is what they would want, him, and the Faerie Queen.

When the piper plays 'Danny Boy' I remind him that they are Scots, not Irish and I bid the man play 'A Scottish Soldier'.

***

It is twenty-five years since I was first imprisoned, for crimes I did not perform, for sins I did not commit.

I have paid the piper many times over.

CHAPTER 43
ARCHANGEL

IT IS MORNING and I have closed the window.

My pet dragon is sitting on a completed manuscript, coyly looking at me as if it is time to feed it.

I gather up the papers and I walk out into the corridor of the apartments.

In other rooms, I can hear people living. The building is suffused with the glow of it.

Sometimes, when the people come to their windows, I can see the dragons they keep with them. And some of the other things too. There is talk among the *kin* of vengeance. They think dark thoughts of blood.

I can see in the scars, borne by these dragons of self, the harm that is occasioned by the suppression of righteous anger, the lack of power to say, 'No. No more. This far and no further.'

Without that power, harm builds up and sticks to people. They carry it around with them, burdened by it, and we are the world we carry with us. The burdens we bear.

I am leaving the house and taking with me a stack of papers prepared by Eddy.

In a moment, I will travel to a church where I have persuaded the Father to provide us a room.

In that room, I will read out a letter that contains all of the secrets Eddy has been carrying, all that he has kept silent, all the burdens of others he has borne.

The Young Queen, to her credit, will listen. She will draw her breath in sharply when she realises Eddy has been eternal witness.

She will attempt to deflect her lover's presence a second time in her life, but Eddy knows better. He knows what is really going on, for Eddy *sees*.

He is her Little Bird.

Eddy has not long been back from his travels, and this is still part of his journey. He will read this letter and cry, and then absolve her, forgive her. She will attempt to rationalise some of this with him, but he is beyond that.

I sit with my hand upon his shoulder until the priest, listening through a crack in the door and terrified of the outcome, walks in and blesses them both.

The Young Queen will call out to Eddy as he leaves. He does not look back.

For the rest of the day, animals will follow him. A dog will jump into the Lane Cove River in front of him and remain, despite its owner's furious request.

'I don't know what got into him,' the owner will say.

Birds will alight on the roof of his car and refuse to move. Eddy has entered a state of grace.

In the *Here-and-Now*, Eddy takes the letter he has written to his mother and burns it, standing in the courtyard of the church he does not believe in but she does.

The letter perishes in fire, to become a shroud of grey, the blue lines on which he has written his ten thousand lives now a faint stripe, the pen marks an even paler grey. The wind catches it and lifts it up over the rooftops of Oxford Street, and it breaks away into small pieces.

The End

THANK YOU

First and foremost, Rooftops owes a debt of gratitude to Suzanne Karolis, who held my hand and walked with me through every line.

Thanks also to Kamaia Harkness and Lucie Ataya for their tremendous editing work, and to the great group of readers and peers who helped and encouraged me during the process.

Thank you to all the survivors who have shared their own stories with me.

Thank you Uncle JD for helping me make sure my approach to indigenous themes was appropriate.

And wherever you are, whatever realms you travel, to my friend, the poet Rick Lyons, thank you.

ABOUT THE AUTHOR

Born and raised in Sydney, Michael Barry is a multimedia artist, songwriter, composer, screenwriter and a volunteer counsellor for trauma.

This is his first novel.